James Rhoades

Timoleon; a dramatic poem

James Rhoades

Timoleon; a dramatic poem

ISBN/EAN: 9783337304409

Printed in Europe, USA, Canada, Australia, Japan

Cover: Foto ©Andreas Hilbeck / pixelio.de

More available books at **www.hansebooks.com**

TIMOLEON:

A DRAMATIC POEM.

BY

JAMES RHOADES.

HENRY S. KING & CO., LONDON.

1875.

TO HER,

WHOSE SWEET NAME LIVING

SHOULD HAVE GRACED THIS MOURNFUL PAGE,

To my Wife

ON THE OTHER SIDE OF DEATH

I DEDICATE THIS

AND ALL MY FUTURE WORK,

WITH THE LOVE THAT IS DEATHLESS.

The Persons.

———◆◇◆———

TIMOLEON.

DEMARISTE, mother of Timophanes and Timoleon.

ÆSCHYLUS, brother to the wife of Timophanes.

ORTHAGORAS, a Soothsayer.

DIONYSIUS, Tyrant of Syracuse.

DIOGENES of Sinope.

DEINARCHUS
DEMARETUS
NEON } Generals under Timoleon.
ISIAS

LYSIAS, a Soldier.

The Furies.

The Ghost of TIMOPHANES.

The Curse of DEMARISTE.

The Spirit of Liberty.

Corinthian Citizens, etc.

Corinthian Women.

Corinthian Soldiers.

Greek Mercenaries of TIMOLEON.

Greek Mercenaries of HIKETAS.

Syracusan Citizens.

Archons.

Heralds.

Chorus of Syracusan Women.

HISTORICAL PREFACE.

TIMOLEON was the son of noble Corinthian parents,
Timodemus and Demariste. The elder son Timophanes
was in all, save personal prowess, the reverse of his
brother, being weak, licentious, and of immoderate
ambition : nevertheless Timoleon loved him dearly, and
to save his life in battle had once jeoparded his own.
About the year 364 B.C., the Corinthians having reason
to suspect foul play from Athens, their ally, resolved to
set on foot a force of four hundred Mercenaries, whom
they equipped and quartered in the citadel under the
command of Timophanes. But this traitor, turning to
the detriment of Corinth the means entrusted to him for
her defence, seized and slew certain of the chief inhabitants, and forthwith proclaimed himself absolute ruler of
the city. Now Timoleon's love for his brother was
strong, but his hatred of tyrants was stronger ; so, when
he heard what was done, he went out to seek Timophanes,

with two friends, Orthagoras, a soothsayer, and Æschylus, brother of the tyrant's wife, in the hope of persuading him to repentance and voluntary atonement for his crime ; but their arguments and entreaties were met first with scorn and then with threats of violence ; till at length, no remedy being left but one, Timoleon with grief and sorrow gave the sign, and these three fell upon Timophanes, and dispatched him. The greater part of the citizens extolled Timoleon for this deed, but some reviled him as a murderer, and loudest among these his own mother, who called down the most dreadful curses on his head. Overwhelmed with the weight of this malediction, he would have put an end to his life ; but, being forcibly dissuaded by his friends, he withdrew to a country retreat near Corinth, where he lived in solitude and dejection for a space of twenty years.

At the end of this time he was called upon to lead the arms of Corinth against another tyrant, Dionysius the younger of Syracuse. This man in the tenth year after his expulsion by Dion had returned and re-established himself in power ; but so intolerable was his license and oppression, that the chief citizens appealed for protection in their misery to Hiketas, despot of Leontini, who, for his own selfish ends, complied with the request, and led an army against Dionysius. In the midst of this trouble a Carthaginian fleet appeared before

Syracuse, which raised the terror of the people to such a pitch, that they sent off an embassy to Corinth, the mother city, to beg assistance. Hiketas also joined publicly in this petition, the better to cloak his real design ; while secretly he treated with the Carthaginians, thinking by the aid of their forces to oust Dionysius, and afterwards divide the city with them.

Meanwhile, the Corinthians having voted to send a force to Syracuse, no general could be found who cared to lead it, until a voice in the assembly proposed Timoleon. A messenger was immediately despatched to him ; the offered post was accepted ; and with seven triremes and one thousand men—the most that could be mustered for so perilous an enterprise—the lonely recluse set forth to be the saviour of Sicily.

Upon his arrival at Rhegium the villany of Hiketas was revealed : for there met him twenty Carthaginian ships with envoys from that prince on board, who gave out that the war being now nearly ended, his help was superfluous, and bade him go no farther. Timoleon feigned submission to this insult, but by an artifice contrived to detain the Carthaginian commanders within Rhegium, while his galleys put to sea, and crossing the strait safely, arrived at Tauromenium. After a few days he surprised and defeated a part of the forces of Hiketas near Adranum, which city opened its gates to him forthwith.

Hereupon Dionysius, who was holding the citadel of Ortygia against Hiketas and the Carthaginians, offered to surrender to Timoleon, stipulating only for permission to pass the remainder of his days undisturbed in Corinth. The condition was allowed; Dionysius was conducted to Corinth; and four hundred men under Neon were sent to garrison Ortygia, Timoleon himself retiring to Katana, to await reinforcements.

Hiketas now summoned to his aid the whole power of Carthage, and Mago shortly arrived with one hundred and fifty ships and a land force computed at sixty thousand.

The Corinthians in Ortygia had much ado to hold the citadel against so numerous a foe; and, being strictly blockaded, they must soon have been starved into submission, had not Timoleon succeeded in sending unobserved through the enemy's fleet some small ships laden with corn from Katana. To put a stop to this, Hiketas and Mago advanced upon Katana with the best of their troops; but during their absence Neon fell upon the remnant with such vigour, that he expelled the besiegers from Achradina, which he thenceforth occupied together with Ortygia. Hiketas and Mago, on hearing it, abandoned their design against Katana, and returned to those quarters of Syracuse which still remained to them.

Neon had thus furnished himself with abundant provisions, and Timoleon too was approaching with reinforcements sent from Corinth.

At this critical juncture, owing partly to the late disasters, and partly to the familiarity which he saw subsisting between the soldiers of Hiketas and those of Timoleon during the intervals of fighting, Mago conceived a suspicion that Hiketas was betraying him, and suddenly withdrew his fleet and army.

This defection so facilitated Timoleon's attack, and so discouraged the troops of Hiketas, that the Corinthians took the town without the loss of a single man. Hiketas escaped to Leontini.

Timoleon, thus master of Syracuse, proved at once his singleness of purpose by summoning the citizens to aid him in pulling down the stronghold of Ortygia. On its site was built a court of justice. This done, with the aid of the Corinthians at home he caused the Syracusan exiles to be recalled from far and near; and, these proving insufficient for the renovation of the community, colonists were invited from other Grecian cities, who swelled the total number of immigrants to sixty thousand. From this may be imagined the desolation which had come upon Syracuse; and the like was true of other towns in Sicily also, where the tyrants reigned; for the inhabitants would fly to the fields or anywhither, rather than remain subject to their oppressors in the cities.

Meanwhile, with the advice of experienced statesmen from home, Timoleon remodelled the constitution upon a free basis, improved their legislation, and allotted the lands and houses of Syracuse to its new inhabitants.

But Hiketas was not yet crushed. At his urgent appeal, a host of seventy thousand men, including all the best native warriors of Carthage, magnificently armed, was despatched under Hasdrubal and Hamilcar, and landed at Lilybæum. To oppose this vast armament Timoleon could only muster a force of about seven thousand men; and even this was diminished on the march by the mutinous flight of a thousand Mercenaries, whose pay was somewhat in arrears. Timoleon, affecting to regard the desertion of these cowards as a gain, pushed forward, and reached the top of the heights above the river Krimesus, while the enemy was still engaged in crossing. Inspired by his voice, which sounded more than human on that day, his infantry charged down the hill, and after vain efforts to break the ponderous masses opposed to them with their spears, got to close quarters with the sword. The unwieldy ranks of the Carthaginians, thus taken at disadvantage, had begun to fall thick and fast, when a terrific storm bursting full upon their faces filled them with superstitious terror, and completed their discomfiture. Ten thousand of them were slain, and the camp was abandoned to the victors, containing an enormous treasure.

Timoleon now marched against Hiketas, who was delivered into his hands alive, and by him executed; and, after speedily restoring to freedom the few remaining cities that were still oppressed by tyrants,* he returned finally to Syracuse, and laid down his power, because his task was done.

In excuse for his retirement from public life he is said to have pleaded the approach of that blindness which shortly after overtook him. Plutarch adds that to the joy and pride of the Syracusans he chose to spend his remaining days with them; and that whenever questions of difficulty arose in the assembly, "he was conveyed in a litter to the theatre," where, after the acclamations of the people had subsided, "he took cognizance of the affair, and delivered his opinion," which generally obtained their sanction: he was then carried out in the same manner, amidst loud applause.

Four or five years after the battle of Krimesus, Timoleon died. His funeral, which was sumptuously conducted at the public expense, was followed by a vast crowd, not only of Syracusans, but of men and women

* For the sake of dramatic order and proportion, these events have been treated in the poem as though they had preceded, instead of following, the victory of Krimesus.

from neighbouring cities "in the most pompous so-
lemnity, crowned with garlands and clothed in white ;"
and the herald made proclamation concerning him as
follows : "The people of Syracuse inter Timoleon the
Corinthian, the son of Timodemus, at the public expense
of two hundred minæ ; they honour him moreover
through all time with annual games, to be celebrated
with performances in music, horse-racing, and wrestling,
as the man who destroyed tyrants, repeopled great
cities which lay desolate, and restored to the Sicilians
their laws and privileges." *

* The passages quoted are from "Langhorne's Plutarch's Lives,"
from which, and from "Grote's History of Greece," the above account
of these events is mainly taken.

TIMOLEON:

𝔄 Dramatic Poem.

AUTHOR'S ERRATA.

Page 23, line 17.   After 'thing,' omit – .

„   24,   „   9.   For 'yet,' read 'well.'

„   24,   „   18.   For 'all, professing,' read 'all-professing.'

„   50,   „   8.   For 'travailèd,' read 'travailed.'

„   71,   „   13.   Before 'some,' insert 'Their last.'

„   90,   „   17.   For 'brokeng,' read 'broken.'

The intestine sore of home-bred tyranny ;
Therefore abroad much dreaded, therefore too
Much loved of all her children, of none more
Than me, who have known and loved her from a child.
Yes, yonder proud pile is the citadel,
Acrocorinthus southward on sheer rock,
High o'er the sister-seas.   I am not mad,

2

from neighbouring cities "in the most pompous so-
lemnity, crowned with garlands and clothed in white;"
and the herald made proclamation concerning him as
follows : "The people of Syracuse inter Timoleon the
Corinthian, the son of Timodemus, at the public expense
of two hundred minæ ; they honour him moreover

TIMOLEON:

A Dramatic Poem.

ACT I.

SCENE I.—*A Street in Corinth.*

TIMOLEON.

[Pacing up and down with an air of perplexity.]

I AM Timoleon the Corinthian, this
Corinth, my native city, blest of heaven,
In that no foreign arm her fort profanes
With hostile occupation, nor—worse ill,
Since harder to be quelled—exhausts her life
The intestine sore of home-bred tyranny;
Therefore abroad much dreaded, therefore too
Much loved of all her children, of none more
Than me, who have known and loved her from a child.
Yes, yonder proud pile is the citadel,
Acrocorinthus southward on sheer rock,
High o'er the sister-seas.   I am not mad,

Bemocked of all my senses, nor asleep,
No, nor yet risen a pale perturbèd shade,
To scare the living, from the uncharnelled dead ;
These are the same broad hands have slain or saved
In rout and onset many a friend or foe:
Why, then, what ails me?—Let me say it again,
I am Timoleon, this my native Corinth,
These all my neighbours, wont to greet me fair
With kind 'good morrow,' and chat i' th' market-place,
As free folk will, of politics and war,
Then sigh for our poor sister Syracuse,
And call God's curse on tyrants.   Now all's changed
In a night, as though some foul usurping dream,
That morning should have murdered, braved it out
Into broad day, and clothed the waking world
Of substance with its lying livery.
God wot, I am not Dionysius,
To flay to-morrow whom I feast to-day,
And trim the scale of State too high for men
By sinking manhood to below the beasts :
And yet my friends, when I would question them
What all this turmoil argues, rush me past
With chalky faces, seeming not to hear.
Why, were the pest on them from door to door
So fierce as erst on Athens, when the dead
Ousted the quick and rotted as they fell,

They would have told me ; or were Athens herself
The plague that lowers upon us, a black cloud
Of treachery, whose big drops are bristling spears,
They would not yet deal so with an old friend,
To lock the secret from me.   I must know
The truth—what makes us strangers ; and indeed
Hither there speeds who from his face should seem
Bursting with eager news—my brother's kinsman,
Æschylus !   Now pray heaven *he* prove not dumb !

ÆSCHYLUS.

Timoleon here !—a loiterer !—hast not heard ?

TIMOLEON.

No, nor can guess, unless the Gods have struck
Corinth with general madness, or transformed
Me to the body of a beast, that none
Of my old friends should know me ; but since thou
Still tak'st me for a man, cease gaping, speak ;
Solve me the riddle.

ÆSCHYLUS.

Hast thou not heard—thy brother—
The chief men slain—riots in the citadel,
Tyrant of Corinth ?—Now canst understand ?

TIMOLEON.

Thy words pass through mine ears, and stun my brain,
But leave no record of intelligence.

ÆSCHYLUS.

'Thus fares the seaman when he strikes, but soon
Recovering sense gets heart to shout for aid,
Or thrust from shore, or bale the settling ship,
So heaven may help him at his pinch.

TIMOLEON.

                      Say'st thou
'Tyrant?   Timophanes!—My mother's son!

ÆSCHYLUS.

My sister's husband!   At the dead of night,
When all good citizens were fast in sleep,
Damn'd treason was awake, ay and abroad;
With those four hundred mercenaries, men
Kept by the State in his command to watch
'Gainst outward wiles, he murdered in their beds,
Unable to suspect a fall so deep,
The chief of those who named him; then at dawn,
High on the shoulders of the cut-throat crew,
Was trumpeted forth despot.—Whither now?
Push not the event so fast: there is much need
We were deliberate in what's left to do.

TIMOLEON.

I go to entreat him, and, despite himself,
Win him to virtue and his saner mind:
May be 'tis not too late; the thought of power

Full oft is sweeter than the taste : already
He surfeits of his sin : experience breeds
Hate in one moment of a life's desire.
Try we persuasion first ; perchance even now
He knows how barren and how bleak it is
To stand unlov'd, unhonour'd, and alone
Upon the frozen tops of sovereignty.

ÆSCHYLUS.

First shall the rain wash cool red Etna's throat,
Ere mild words melt a tyrant in his ire.

TIMOLEON.

Nay, he will hear me : thou rememberest how,
That dreadful day, six hours of fighting o'er,
Our weaker wing fell back before the weight
Of Argos and Cleonæ : he was down
Among the horse-hoofs, blinded with his blood,
And stunned with blows ; a score of troopers rushed
With lowering spears to make an end of him,
When I, from out the foot-men, seeing it, ran,
Bestrode his body, and bore him safe away,
Myself, too, sorely wounded, and my targe
Thick-planted with a copse of quivering steel—
I shall prevail with him for that day's sake.

ÆSCHYLUS.

And if thou failest, then ?

TIMOLEON.

O Æschylus !

He was my brother, my own mother's son !
But if his heart relent not——come away.

Chorus.

With trembling steps from out the neighbour-street,
  Consumed with fear as with a fire,
   Hurrying I heard
A sound, a voice, that made my heart to beat,
  And both ears tingle with desire,
   A glorious word.
  But irresistible in man
The inborn lust of power and of oppression
Springs, and takes root, and strikes as deep as hell,
  Choking each pure and chastened thought,
   Each holier passion,
That in the meek submissive mind doth dwell
By prayer and sober vigilance unwrought :
As some vast yew in a dark mountain-dell,
   Alone since years began,
   Immovable, immutable,
Inexorable, in overweening pride
   Spares not to spurn aside,
   Starved from the kind earth's womb,
Each dwarfish flower that sickens at its feet
   In uncongenial gloom,

No, not for any intercession,
From morning-tide till even-tide,
Of bitter skies or sweet,
Of sun, or rain, or equal airs that fan,
Or shine, or fall,
Alike on all.
Yea, ev'n though at his birth he may inherit,
Through fate's mysterious plan,
The flower of all the earth for his possession,
Riches beside, and wisdom, ay and merit,
Beauty and wit to please,
Yet be content with these,
Except his power be throned for men to fear it,
His robe be edged with hate for him to wear it,
He neither will nor can.
So was it with the ancient stock
Of Sisyphus and Cypselus,
That of Æolian, this of Dorian strain ;
The Dionysian vulture ravins thus
Upon the well-loved isle,·
Our home, we left erewhile
Across the main :
Now in a strange land lights the curse on us,
Ne'er to be lifted from our necks again,
Unless the tyrant shall be taught
By some insuperable shock,

Or not in vain
Warned by the everlasting pain
Of Sisyphus to set his pride at naught,
Nor give to lewd desires too loose a rein.
Oh ! that in the deep there were,
Or above the starry skies,
Refuge for the wanderer
Out of sight of all men's eyes !
Far away from all men's voices,
In some silent paradise
Broken by no ruder noises
Than the low melodious singing
Of the nymph as she arises
From the fountain ever springing
At our feet, while far above
In blue ether softly winging
Floats the Cytherean dove ;
Where the minstrel to his lyre
Tells no harsher tale than love,
And no heart with fiercer fire
Burns, nor lights with emulation
Of immoderate desire.
Never king from all creation
Reigned there, nor the lord of war
Fell like night upon the nation
Scared with thunders of his car ;

None whose feet are stained with slaughter
Pass there, nor the lips that are
Lovers of delirious laughter
O'er the wine-cup's mad excess,
But such cheer as earth's glad daughter
Brings the reaping-folk to bless,
After sojourn long returning
From dark Hades, none the less
Fills each heart with tender yearning,
With sedate and holy pleasure
Hated of the undiscerning ;
Where no lust of hoarded treasure
Tempts the sailor o'er the seas
To forsake love, home, and leisure,
For the stormy Cyclades,
Of past ills insatiate,
Till a darker chance than these
Finds him, and he learns too late
Wisdom when he comes to die,
And his house stands desolate.
Whoso keeps before his eye
Sober aims, and in his mind
Blest contentment, him will I
Praise, whatever Fates be kind,
Whatso cruel ; but, for me,
Careless what men lose or find,

One thing lack I yet—to be
Where nor pride nor passion is,
Nor delight, nor misery,
Nor friend's curse, nor traitor's kiss,
Nor hearts sick with vain devotion,
Nor the vain desire of bliss,
And, all hope and all emotion
Ended, as is surely best,
Under earth, beyond the ocean,
Somewhere, somewhere to find rest.

1st Semichorus.

Hark ! did ye hear a sound of lamentation
    Float hither on the south wind tremulously ?

2nd Semichorus.

Again ! and louder ! as the acclamation
    Of them that shout for new-born liberty !

1st Semichorus.

A wail of cities, as when earth is shaken,
    And the sea trembles and the mountains sway !

2nd Semichorus.

A cry of captains, when the towers are taken,
    And men ride onward to divide the prey !

1st Semichorus.

Ah ! did ye hear a dirge of many voices,
    As when they mourn around a dead man's bier ?

2nd Semichorus.

Nay, as the bridegroom with his friends rejoices,
    And the mirth deepens, as the bride draws near.

1st Semichorus.

Hark yet ! a voice of weeping and of cursing
    Red-handed deeds of death-deserving wrong !

2nd Semichorus.

Nay, but a nation its great acts rehearsing,
    With praises and solemnity of song.

1st Semichorus.

Chill trembling holds me, as when night-clouds thicken,
    And no star pricks the horror of the sky.

2nd Semichorus.

Mine eye grows brighter, as the faint hills quicken
    Rejoicing that the dawn is by-and-by.

              [*Enter* ORTHAGORAS.

1st Semichorus.

Say, prophet, what dark tidings hast thou brought,
What dire forebodings big with misery ?

2nd Semichorus.

What present comfort of deliverance wrought,
And what glad promise of good days to be ?

ORTHAGORAS.

Ye ask not vainly, since one day brings forth
A double birth of twin-born hope and fear.

Chorus.

Pray all the right may prosper; but do thou
Unriddle the dark tenor of thy speech.

ORTHAGORAS.

Ladies, have heart, and let the gods be praised;
Uprooted lies the new-blown tyranny.

Chorus.

How sayest thou? sown and withered in a night!
By man's hand vanquished, or the mightier Fates?

ORTHAGORAS.   .

By swift award of following destiny,
As one blood-guilty pays the murderer's debt.

Chorus.

How stricken? or who the executioners?
Prithee, forbear not, but set forth the tale.

ORTHAGORAS.

He fell heart-pierced by a triple blow;
For I, with his bride's brother, Æschylus,
And his own blood, Timoleon, now sole son
Of Demariste, childless otherwise,
Nay childless at this hour, could curses kill,
We three went forth without much hope indeed,
But since Timoleon's love would have it so,
Making assay to bow the tyrant's pride
By stern expostulation. At the foot

Of his new home, the citadel, he met us,
Guarded on either side, in front, behind,
From all foes outward; from his inmost self,
Worst foe of all, unguarded, and the fangs
Of that coiled serpent fattening at his heart.
Timoléon first went forward, with grave eye
Greeting the tyrant; we, some steps withdrawn,
Paused while the brothers met, but spake no word.
Thrice he importuned him with tears and prayers,
That would have moved a multitude, whose eyes
Had never wept before; first by that oath
Sworn to the State: 'the State is dead,' laughed he,
" There is no restitution in the grave."
Next by the loved knees and reverèd head
Of their one mother, and one common blood
Betwixt them twain, a twin fraternal strength
From birth to manhood, never broke till now :—
He stood as one stone-deaf, or as a man
That hears strange language in an alien tongue.
Last he conjured him by the strong compulsion
Of his once rescued life, by that dear debt
Of intense toil and battle-agony,
And blood poured forth like water, to requicken
The stamped-out life of Corinth, and wash clean
Her stainèd honour: otherwise he stood
There to reclaim his gift, adjust the odds

Even to the uttermost inexorably.
This was a summons he could understand;
For the boar-swine at bay, no longer man,
Hissed out defiance 'twixt clenched teeth, and foamed
Infatuate, as the Furies drove him on.
'How, fool!' he shouted, 'think'st thou to outface,
Outbrave, and overbear me by the weight
Of one life's vantage?   Should I spare thee now
Unscathed for this, the paltry debt is paid
A hundred times and over; but have care,
Mouth me no more thy curs'd remembrances
Henceforth: new fashions come with the new day.'
       Then stood Timoleon with averted eyes,
Silent a space and praying: at last he cried,
'Traitor! thy blood be on no head but thine;
The hour is come: to Corinth I devote
The life, would heaven I had not lived to save.'
So, ere the guards could aid him, he was dead;
For we three closed upon him, who speechless, blind,
Trembling with rage intolerable, fell
Dead, as a bull is butchered, heavy as he
And helpless; while the huddling herd behind
Stood stupid, gazing on Timoleon.
Then, as bewitched by Circe's sovereign spell
Or pale Medea's midnight sorceries,
Each at the mute commandment of his eye

Confounded, no word spoken, with one clang
Dropped spear and buckler, all the savage soul
Tamed in them, and the wordy tumult lulled.

    I know not how the general sort may judge
The fact or him; he is above the cast
Of their conjecture: but should Corinth need,
In some strait pass of fortune, one to guide
Safe for the open, or untwist the knots
And tangles of inextricable war,
Let Corinth look to this man, for by heaven!
I´have not known his like.   So, fare you well.

Chorus.

Farewell; but may the gods o'errule the event
To thy forecasting and the hopes of all.

                 [*Exit* ORTHAGORAS.
                 [*Enter* DEMARISTE.

DEMARISTE.

Sicilian women, have ye seen my son?
The accursed, the abominable, who slew,
Not in fair field an open enemy,
Victorious in the chance of blow for blow,
But with base wile, but as a beast is slain
Caught in the toils, unconquerable else,
A mightier and more honourable man,
His brother, chief of Corinth, flower of men,
The first-fruit of my labour?—Woe is me!

Have ye no hearts, that gape on my distress,
Like unfed birds, nor have one word to say?
Oh! brutish, past all utterance! knowing not
The natural human bond of kin to kin!
With his own hand he sought him, with his hand
Slew him, and had no pity. Ah! my son,
First-born of me and goodliest! Have not I—
Ah! yes, how often have I seen, and smiled,
Thee elder in the house, thyself a babe,
With tender uncontrol of tottering feet
Lead him full gently—thy hand clasping his,
His hand that slew thee!   Oh! his eye was kind:
With smiling show of smooth hypocrisy
He sought thee out to kill thee: impious!
With fair speech aping virtue, that beside
His blackness blackest midnight should be noon.
Shall I not rail at heaven? what plague have they
From all their storehouse of fanged agonies,
Red-heapèd horrors of the wrath of God,
What curse, what fiery bolt, what barbèd pang
Unlaunched, that I should fear it—that would not fall
Faint as shed feathers from the snow-cloud's wing,
Soft stars of showery coolness wavering down
Upon some scorch'd and thunder-rifted scalp
Of pine in gorges of Edonian hills?
Oh! me! of all the mothers in all the world

Most miserable ! who having nursed and reared,
Borne of my body, and suckled at my breast,
Two fair men-children to my pride, erewhile
A double flower and crown of married days,
First of the fairest am untimely reft,
Cut off in summer's height, nor next can turn
To my sole prop remaining, but must find
A two-edged monster of devouring hate,
More fell than Scylla or that prodigious seed
Sprung from the blood of Uranus and Ge,
Porphyrion and Alcioneus, or what
Of foul abortive shape dread Perseus slew,
Or that Chimæra, or the envenomed folds
Of hyperboreal Ladon,—worse than these,
Yea, than Orestes' self to her that bare him
More bitter, and a deadlier birth to me.
What have ye left me of sweet, the gods and thou ?
What fruit of life or labour?   Behold, for love
I am filled with loathing, and with despair for hope ;
And all my life falls from me, shaken and shed
From these old boughs ; my name once honourable
Brought to dishonour—my so fruitful house
A desolation—all the cup of wrath
To the last scalding drop and shameful dregs
Poured on my helpless head !   Lo ! here I am,
Stripped bare, cut off, cut down, a barren tree.

Made empty of all desire of all things sweet—
Of all sweet things and bitter, save only this,
Once more to see him that was my bane, once more—
The thrice-defiled, the slayer of all delight—
To see him, and curse him to his face, and die.

Chorus.

Have patience, lady ; in cursing is no cure,
Nor in relentless wrath a remedy.

DEMARISTE.

What profit then hath patience, or what part
Honour with infamy, or I with thee?

Chorus.

Not first art thou to suffer, and with mad words
Whet more the edge of thine own suffering.

DEMARISTE.

There is no sharpening of a woe like mine—
One murdered son, and one the murderer.

Chorus.

All healing is of silence and slow time.

DEMARISTE.

Yet shall one curse his bitterest enemy.

Chorus.

Yea, but a mother her own flesh and blood?

DEMARISTE.

No blood but poison, and no flesh but stone.

                        [*Enter* TIMOLEON.

TIMOLEON.

Mother, most sacred of all names, I come
To deprecate thy curses, not to sue
For pardon, howsoe'er to thee I seem
A sinner, and hateful in thine eyes to-day,
Even of all men most hateful, who was once
Thy son, beloved and blameless. Hear me plead,
Mother, nor stiffen my warm limbs to stone
With the cold gaze of unregardful eyes,
And set face frozen in hate, and firm fierce lips
Locked fast from comfortable words, till now
Soft-moulded to all shapes of tender speech.
What shall I say? thou knowest my heart, my hand,
Thou knowest I loved and slew him: knowest thou why?
Nay, for thou shrink'st as from a loathly thing,
And in thy soul unnatural hate is more
Than thy most natural sorrow. As for me,
My blood, one throb of burning agony,   .
Feels yet no prick of shame: for Corinth's sake,
Because his mind was set on villanies,
And his heart travailed of a deadly thing,
And his hand wrought it ; because he took to bride
Power, and gat death to first-born, and with death

3 *

Ambition, monstrous enemy of man,
Falsehood, and fraud, and every vice of kings;
Because he widened his desires as hell,
And would not hear entreatment, but waxed vile,
And made his lust insatiate as the sea,
And from a healing and a help became
A common curse to country, home, and kin,—
Because of all these things, for Corinth's sake,
Yea, therefore, mother, for thy sake and mine,
I did not fear to slay him.   But oh ! ye heavens,
Oh ! fates, how crossly have ye drawn the threads
Athwart my web of life, to tangle it !
Not only visiting the contentious man,
Stiff-necked, and insolent of hand and tongue,
Ye smite his heart with blindness, step by step
Lured on to new precipitous heights of sin,
Till he shoot over to some dreadful deep
Through the void yawn of unsustaining air,
But him too who with lowly reverent mind
On life's firm level plants a steadfast foot,
And swerves not from the right, him too ye draw
On to the same red pit, as me ye have drawn,
And for no sin of mine have made my name
An execration, and this guiltless hand
Polluted, even in its most righteous act
Of retribution, with the kindred blood

Of one far dearer than myself to me.
Oh ! misery piled on misery mountains high !
Too vast a heft for Atlas, yet all heaped
On the weak pillars of one human heart !
Surely the happiest life is sad enow,
So brief of term, so bitter in event—
So many reefs and currents of the soul,
Opposing passions, contrary desires !
An even course 'twixt either foul extreme
So hard to compass, till the port be won !
But whoso in the quest of worldly gain
Makes shipwreck, or, for pleasure voyaging,
Upon some unforeseen calamitous rock
Falls foundered, losing all, though him the world
Count miserable, yet did he never seek
The highest, and hath not lost it ; and e'en he
Full oft, with life escaping, timely warned,
May shape new aims, refit his shattered bark,
And, bound on some more moderate just emprise,
Pluck golden vantage from adversity.
But I have no such hope, not having fallen
Through mine own fault or folly, who never yet
In all the journey of my days divorced
Discretion from my steps, nor hurled at heaven
Great swelling words of arrogance, nor strained
Between uplifted lips to take and taste

The high-hung fruits of honour : and yet behold me
Sunk down more hopelessly in deeper mire,
And suffering deadlier defeat than he !
Are the gods just that plague their worshippers,
And for lip-service and the bended knee,
And life-long adoration of pure hearts,
Alike to guiltless and to guilty mete
One measure of life to all, one dole of death ?
Or do they move by paths fortuitous,
Or bond-slaves to inexorable law
Leave men perforce to perish ?—Black thought, away !
Duty is best, though hell come after it,
And heaven is far, and no man knows the end.
Out on my weak lamentings, making vile
The serene air of silent suffering !
Unworthy of me ! unworthy of a man,
Who still hath striven before all aims to find
His sole advancement in the general good !
Whoso to fatherland himself hath given,
What need hath he of lowlier happiness
Or lesser loves beside it? or what sorrow
Can shake him from that service, to disown
For narrower ties his heart's allegiance?

   Mother, let not these red and tear-scarred eyes
Deceive thee : do not herein think to read
Weak traces of repentance ; I rejoice

That I had strength to do it, had strength to leap
At once, not girl-like on the awful edge
Hang shuddering, but as some storm-fed stream
Spills in an instant over with one bound,
Clear from the cliff : yea, mother, I rejoice ;
It was the dark necessity, not the deed,
That rent my soul asunder—yet, ah ! yet,
If any power could change me or compel,
Check my impetuous current, turn my tide,
And hurl me back rebellious on myself,
Mother, thy curse would do it; if any prayers
Move me, thy face beseeching ; if any thought,
Surely the thought of thy past tenderness
And love of old time.   Nay, what idle words !
Thou knowest how I have held thee all my days
Dearest of all things living, and after thee
Him, and have deemed my life a common thing,—
If therewith I might serve you or save from shame,
So set my heart to you-ward : now all this
Is nothing, and lo ! some god has sent a cloud
To rest between us, and darkened our delight,
That whatso' wave of fate roll in, at least
We have done with happiness, we two I think
For ever.   Let us bid farewell to joy
Now dead and buried; yet, if thou judge me right,
We need not part from honour, but take her home

To be our chiefest and most cherished guest
On the empty throne of pleasure ; and she shall bring
Fair peace, that is her fellow ; and we may live
To comfort each the other ; and Corinth too,
Our country, with her favour shall almost
Make light the burden of impending hours,
And with her benediction, when we die,
Console us, who have suffered for her sake.

DEMARISTE.

Snake ! thou art subtle-tongued, but yet I know
What venom, for all the musical sweet hiss,
Lurks in thy lying and detested mouth.
Think'st thou to lure me too with honied words,
Monster ! fresh-taught by thy most hideous act,
Then shut me in the dark of horrid jaws,
One more unnatural victim ?   Out, vile worm !
Crawl hence, lest my foot crush thee in thy slime !
Nay, an' thou wilt have answer, thou shalt hear :
O virtuous, all, professing hypocrite !
O spider, hanging from thy dustythreads,
To snare the unwary with fine sophistries !
O specious pseudo-patriot, robed in fair
Tyrannicidal cloak of fratricide !
Most tender cut-throat, who couldst scarcely kill
Thine only brother, so wondrous deep the love
Thou barest him ! have thou thy meed of me.

Because thou art traitor to thy race and name,
Yea, to all kindred of humanity,
Cruel as a beast, flint-hearted, in thy wrath
Most deadly, because thou mad'st thyself a sword
Sheathed in dissimulation, sharp with hate,
To pierce thy brother, and thy lips gaped for him
And hot tongue thirsted till it drank his blood,
Therefore behold !   I, Demariste, I
The womb that bare thee and the breasts that reared,
The hands that nursed thee on my knees, the lips
That sang above thee sleeping, or hushed thy cry
With low sweet murmur of fond foolish words,
I and all these in me do here revoke
Each tender office, and bid thee take instead
A mother's malediction : be thou cursed,
As now thou art hated, as all springs of love
Are dried between us, and all sweet memories
Past like the shadow of a bird in heaven.

        [*Exit* DEMARISTE.

1st Semichorus.

Lo, women's love for strength is as the sea,
And as vexed waters inconsolable.

2nd Semichorus.

But their wrath kindled is as raging fire
Before them, and men's hearts stubble and dry wood.

TIMOLEON.

I pray you, friends, be pitiful to her,
That hath much need of pity, and be not harsh
Or hasty of judgment upon her and me,
As though we had sinned of our own wilfulness
Each against other.   But these things are not so.
Believe me of her whom late ye heard so curst,
So stormy of speech, proud and implacable,
No woman once in oregentle, no voice more mild,
Eyes full of meekness yoked with majesty,
Fondness with grave restraint.   That was not she
Lightening and thundering in our eyes and ears;
Whom sorrow hath severed from herself, till lo !
Even as her love was once, so now her hate.
But witness, O ye gods ! I have not moved
Of my own will to grieve her, that no power
Less than omnipotent necessity
Had spurred me to that deed.   I do not boast
The filial piety of past days—no more
Than merest acts of duty : nay, despite
Most bitter curses I am still constrained
To love her ; such a debt of tender care,
But half-remembered and requited never,
Even over and above the natural bond,
Man owes to her that bare him.

　　　　　　　　　　Now I go

Hence with my griefs upon me : nevermore,
Corinth, in thy dear streets shall I be seen
Among the eager crowds that throng thy quays,
On traffic bent or pleasure—never more
Go forth, loved city, when the trumpet sounds
To onset from thy walls, and the sun strikes
On spear and helmet; but far hence, alone,
Girt with intolerable woes I bend
My steps, an exile, with one hope, to be
Forgotten, oh ! how blest, might I forget !
And so farewell, and of your courtesy
Pray you be pitiful to her and me.

[*Exit* TIMOLEON.

Chorus.

O dark, strange, swift,
Unfathomable mystery,
Thought-baffling, sight-outsoaring,
Of life's vicissitude !
Past man's imagination
The endless alternation,
Wherewith light mortals drift
In helpless misery
From good to ill—from ill again to good,
Over the waves of Fate,
And think to find for their imploring

Some quiet anchorage,
Safe from the tempest's rage,
When these abate,
Or on dry land a refuge from its roaring.

Alack ! for who shall turn a page
Of that sealed book voluminous,
Which lies
Within the shadowy lap of Destiny,
And marks the term of each of us,—
Stern chronicler of hours and days,—
And who 'neath Fortune's foot shall prostrate lie,
And who shall rise
Uncrushed by her rude buffetings,
Superior to all praise ?

There is no revelation of these things
From heaven, nor any end descried
Far off to earth's perplexity,
Nor any law to walk thereby,
Nor any light to guide :
The fierce brunt of outrageous opposites
Alarms on every side,
And with strange contraries
Mocks old experience,
Confounds all evidence,

And fools the wisest and most practised sights.
And one that loves himself, and longs to live
    Heaped round with golden luxuries,
    And lacking time alone to thrive,
    Dies on an instant presently ;
    And one long weary of his breath,
      With battle-toil forspent,
Or by cross blows of rudest accident
        Crushed utterly,
 Cries in his anguish upon death,
      And cannot die.

      Wherefore 'tis meet
That ye refrain the abundance of your lips
    From all vain overflow,
With temperate outcome of sharp words or sweet,
Seeing that the ends of Fate shall no man know ;
    For loud words lash like whips,
Quick to recoil upon the utterer,
    With backward-biting blow.
    Bold deeds let no man grudge,
But bold speech, being barren of all men's thanks,
    Bears fruit alone of sin :
    Right vain it is to judge ;
Even as in battle for a bystander
Word-victory is no whit hard to win :

But if one stand amid the ranks,
　　When the arrow of unseen Fate comes hurtling in,
　　Who knows if he shall budge ?

Nathless we are sure, what else soe'er be taken,
　　　　And shut from sight,
There is that in all tempests shines unshaken,
　　　　A deathless light :
Who in prosperity being meek of spirit,
　　　　And clean of hands,
When the storm bursts on him is strong to bear it,
　　　　Rock-rooted stands,
And in the hurricane and most fierce commotion,
　　　　Of cataract skies,
Dares all its horrors with unquenched devotion,
　　　　Unflinching eyes,
Saith to the storm-fiend, ' Though thy name be legion,
　　　　Haste here to dwell,
Howl, and possess you your appointed region,
　　　　My heart, your hell : '
To the lithe lightning, " Cease dumb rocks to shiver,
　　　　Shoot here, for I
Fear not the emptying of thy fiery quiver,
　　　　But fear to lie ; "
Who 'gainst all tides of tyrannous aggression,
　　　　Strikes manfully,

Naked beneath the strong man's armed oppression,
      Ne'er bowed the knee,
Shoots not defiance from proud lips profaning
      Heaven's sovereign will,
Over himself and his own heart's complaining
      Victorious still,
His name posterity shall set up for token
      In doubtful days,
Him with songs sung or of the heart unspoken
      Shall all men praise.

ACT II.

SCENE I.—*Timoleon's Solitary Retreat near Corinth.*
After a lapse of twenty years.
TIMOLEON.

THEE first, high Lord of heaven, eternal Zeus,
The Saviour-God, I supplicate, and next
Themis, Olympian Justicer supreme,
Sprung from the primal earth ; and I invoke
Dark Hecate, and the stupendous brows
Of Hades, and, coheirs of endless night,
Demeter mother and pale Persephone,
Thrones of the under-world.   But chiefly thou,
Apollo, Purifier, thou Lord of light
And order, the bright bringer of the day,
Who for the Python slain erewhile didst vail
Thy godhead to the unconquerable king,
Thou who of old didst intercede to save
From the everlasting doom thy worshipper
Orestes, and didst cleanse him of a spot
More heinous, and blood shed at thy behest—
Have mercy, hearken, and judge my cause and me.
Nay, Lord, thou knowest; thine universal eye,
That sweeps the immeasurable arc of heaven,

Beheld me from the first, and twice ten years—
Slow-crawling centuries of remorseless pain—
Hath seen me in these unfrequented fields
A sufferer, silent.   I grow gaunt and old,
And my wits craze with sorrow, and all my strength
Crumbles in premature decrepitude :
For I have ta'en a hurt within the soul,
That mocks all medicine of oblivious time,
Dealt by the sword of Fate, that circling seemed
To crown my head with glory before it fell,
Then smote, and brake within me, and grew to be
Bone of my bone, an evil graft of pain,
A wound inveterate, ineradicable.
As when the splendour of a sudden bolt
Splits darkness, and the clouds clap hands to see—
Day dawns, and silence deepens, but the stone
Wedg'd in the wounded heart-strings of the hills
Sticks fast, and cools there, and henceforth becomes
Part of the mountain which it maimed.   Ah, me !
The body's ills how easy to be borne !
Rack, flame, disease, how light, how sufferable,
Match'd with this inward aching of the mind,
That knows no cure, no solace even in thought !
For which way turning shall a soul find rest,
When all the universe is wrapt in storm
Blown from all quarters by all winds at once?

What cloud-break cleaves that sky, what path may save.
Or what roof shelter from its fiery bale ?
But as the outpouring of red Vulcan's wrath
Brims o'er from Ætna, and devastates the plain,
One sulphurous ocean fed by flaming streams,
So 'mid the fierce convulsion of my woe
I seem to float upon a gulf of fire,
Where past and present ills, and ills to be,
Melt altogether, and roll one burning lake
Of indistinguishable agony.
For day by day the irrevocable curse
Of a dead mother, like a blight from heaven,
Blasts me unseen, and all the ghostly troops
Of darkness, grim apparitors of Pain,
Have charge to torture me—mute mouthing shapes,
And incorporeal voices, and I am haled
By hands invisible, that rend my flesh
And pluck me by the beard ; and bat-like things,
Abominations spawn'd of Stygian slime,
With blood-stained talons and plumes dipped in hell,
Float past, and flap me with their inky vans.
But even these haste with hideous croak dismay'd
In some dark den to hide them, at the approach
Of that blood-freezing horror and threefold pest
The Furies, daughters of primeval Night.
Shaped woman-wise are they with scales for skin,

Monstrous ! black-bodied, but of pale fungus-hue
Their faces; and from each gaping nostril goes
A poisònous smoke that through the wholesome air
Spreads pestilence before them ; but they run
Bird-footed, and round their clammy shoulders cling—
A moving marvel of portentous hair—
Coiled serpents, as beneath each bristling brow
The loathèd cunning of an aspick's eye
Leers through the sanguine ooze.   So foul to tell,
To sight intolerable, these abhorrèd fiends
With faultless scent track out their human prey,
And rend his soul with fangs invisible.

    Why then live on ? because death's hideousness
Affrights me, or desire of life allures?
Nay, but because, living, a man may cope
With misery, because, while breath remains,
Timoleon is not bondsman to despair:
Because one thought sustains me, that ye gods
Live, and that Justice tarries, but is not dead,
Nor fiend nor fury shall avail to damn
Whom his own heart upbraids not—but to die,
Self-driven a shadow to the realm of shades,
Were to fling conquest to these hounds of hell,
And sate their malice everlastingly.

    But hark ! methought e'en now their ravenous cry
Smote on my wakeful ear: it is the hour

They love to torture me, for all night long
They have fasted, and wax hungry for my pain.
Now vanish for a while the attendant shapes
That are their mute and slavish ministers,
Dreams and dumb horrors, that break up my sleep,
Or make it frightful, that the body's strength,
Worn by long battling with the powers of night,
May tremble at their torments.   Hark ! again,
That savage bay triumphant on the trail !
No help, no hiding ! the accursed spell
Binds me already, and the morning air
Grows faint with their pollution ere they come.

[Enter the Furies.

1st *Fury.*

Once more, Timoleon, from the obscurest pit
Of hell's profound we come to wait on thee,
That have been too long absent.   For thy sake
We have made tireless search, and from a place
So dark that none durst enter it but we,
So foul with noisome vapours, poisonous damps,
Drained through the pores of Tartarus drop by drop,
That we ourselves nigh sickened at the approach,
And Pluto's vaults beside it seemed bright homes
Of air and sunshine, we have groped, and bring
The first-fruit of its garnered floor to thee.

2nd Fury.

Thence, for thy will is stubborn, we return
Armed each with sevenfold horrors—ghastly pangs
Of keen remorse and impotent desires,
Of power to madden the mightiest God that sits
Throned on Olympus. See this dead man's skull,
Half choked with grave-dust that was once the brain !
It is thy brother's ! In that cup we brewed
Last night a juice of magic potency,
That hath distilled a thousand years in hell,
And thou art first to taste it : if one drop
But pass into thy blood along the veins,
Thenceforth the accumulated agonies,
Which else through all thine after-life were spread
And parcell'd by the slow dividing hours,
Concentred in one mass shall fall on thee
That moment and for ever : matched with this
The bitterest hour that yet thy soul hath known,
Since first we triumphed in thy pains, shall seem
An ecstasy of bliss, more sweet than long
Deep slumber in the lap of Paradise.

3rd Fury.

Moreover, that which thy rebellious heart
Yet dreams not of, self-hate and self-reproach
Shall shoot like fire along thy bones, and lick

The life-springs round thy heart, till thou shalt yearn
More madly to escape thy cursèd self,
Than shun the avenging plagues that visit thee.
We shall exult to see thee, and hear thy moans
Grow deeper hour by hour ; for we are they
Whose office is to punish and to purge
The mad breach of inviolable vows,
Rash-handed outrage and unnatural hate,
And loves unlawful, and whatso lifts a foot
To invade the sanctities of home and kin.
Woe to the sinner, upon whose wilful head
We pour the vials of treasured old revenge
For sins inexpiate !   His dear blood of life
Slowly we lap ; nor sleep shall overshade,
Nor wine-cup cheer him ; hungry he shall heap
The board with dainties, and yet loathe to taste ;
His thoughts shall sting like hornets ; till at last
From sheer amazement and distraction dire
No flight shall save him, and no God redeem.
Next, to the State partaker of his curse,
Unshrived of its pollution, we mete out
Rapine and lust and blood, all ills that spring
From hot swift acts of vengeance : then we drink
The shrieks of flaming cities, which fierce kings
Sack for their pastime, and unseen ride on
Upon the whirlwind above battling hosts,

To mad men's hearts with slaughter.   Yea, no less,
When mounting Virtue from some envious height
Down-toppling swings into the blank abyss,
We spare not, nor we pity ; but as it rolls,
And plunging feels the sickening void beneath,
We loose each barrier, close each mouthèd chasm,
Which else had hushed the thunder of its course
But half-way down to ruin.   So Fate awards,
And Justice elder than the primal heavens.
Therefore behold ! our jealous watch we keep
Each morn by thee, the last grim forfeiture
Of life foretasting, as through finer pangs
Sifted we mark thee dwindling to despair,
Yet in thy fall defiant.   O vain worm !
Say must we teach thee with worse whips and stings,
Or wilt thou yield thee to the all-taming yoke,
And hie with us to hell, where thou must be
Our thrall and liegeman ?   Lo ! what profits more
Thy stubborn tarriance ? for the hot blood-smell
Smokes in our nostrils, and the days on earth
Suffice not, till we measure out thy doom.

TIMOLEON.

Vile hags, the sight of you alone is hell,
And hell to suffer at your cursed decrees,
And smart beneath your scourges ; yet know I

One deeper hell that far outfathoms all—
To be yourselves and wield them.

                                    It may be
Sometimes that in the amazement of my woe
Aghast, confounded, blind with agony,
I have raved out mad words of scalding hate
Against the gods, myself, and all the world.
It may be, for I know not ; but know ye
That whatso leaping fires of forked dismay
Rive me and rend, heave and convulse my frame,
Henceforth, let Reason hold her sovereign seat,
In one thing I defy you ; while I live
Ye shall not force my nature from itself
To blast me with your likeness : I shall still
Suffer and hate you, I Timoleon still
Cleave to mine own uprightness : yea, though men
Forget me, and all gods abandon, this
Mine innocency, despite these guilty spots,
Stands like a pillar when the roof-tree falls
In ashes : never shall my burning tongue,
Delirious with your torments, speak one word
Against the majesty of mine own soul,
No nor profane the vilest name on earth
With curses that are consecrate to you.

        Ah ! me, that pang ! I never felt your power.
Loathed ones, till now.   Yon horrid cup still brims

Untasted, yet your menace is fulfilled.
My bulk contains not the tumultuous throes,
That rage and swell for mastery, till methinks
I am transformed to Suffering's self, and pass
Into the being of immortal Pain.
Fiends, ye may laugh ; but at this darkest hour
I faint not ; never further from your clutch
Was victory than now : some prophet-voice
In accents long unwonted whispering
Tells of deliverance nigh ; and I believe
These are the birth-pangs of new hope, that soon—
Ah ! God, these torments ! Help me to endure.

1st *Fury.*

Past prating now ! Come, sister, fetch the cup,
And thou wrench open his white quivering lips,
Whilst like a tender sick-nurse down his throat
I pour the medicine.

2nd *Fury.*

                    That were labour lost :
Wait till he waken from his swoon.

3rd *Fury.*

                                    Ay, wait
That he may taste each drop of bitterness,
And know its utter vileness to the dregs.

Chorus of Furies.

Come, dance we round the victim first; 'tis rapture to
    behold
The toil of our hard hunting crowned at last with victory:
More sweet than flesh of slaughtered swine, or ransom-
    heap of gold,
Is strength that battles with despair, as fire with surging
    sea.

Long-wooed, he yields to us at last: what charms with
    ours can vie?
Spout, fire and smoke! writhe, serpent-locks! let every
    ringlet hiss:
His stifled groans are more to us than lover's softest
    sigh,
Each drop of anguish on his brow more precious than a
    kiss.

The eldest of all gods are we, and sprung from ancient
    Night,
But blacker than our dam the task, stern Fate to us doth
    give,
Who burn with unappeased desire for our eternal right
To tear the guilty after death, and track them while they
    live.

                  [They continue dancing.

[*Enter* ÆSCHYLUS *and* ORTHAGORAS *in the distance.*

ÆSCHYLUS.

The shadow of these trees is strangely dark.

ORTHAGORAS.

Ay, and the air is chill : some sudden fog
Hath muffled up the sun, a moment since
So fierce upon our foreheads.

ÆSCHYLUS.

     Look ! behold him !

ORTHAGORAS.

Where ?

ÆSCHYLUS.

   Stretched beneath yon cypress, whose old roots
Pillow his sunken head ! why, mark you not ?

ORTHAGORAS.

I see the corpse of some poor wayfarer
By age and misery hunted to this spot,
Where both have left him.

ÆSCHYLUS.

     Know you not that brow ?
And see ! the wan lips move, as though he prayed
In a great agony.   Keep we close awhile,
And tarry till he rise or speak to us.

Chorus of Furies.

We thirst not for the righteous blood ; and those whom
    headlong sin
By sudden storm of frenzy blown athwart our toils hath
    cast,
Even such through purifying pains and lustral fires may
    win
Deliverance of the avenging ones found merciful at last.

But who with rash rebellious hand and mad deliberate
    mind
Hath seized the helm of violence and struck the shoals
    of shame,
The curse, that was before the world, about his neck we
    bind,
Nor know we any younger god shall ease him of the
    same.

The clear light of his soul shall wane and wither in
    eclipse ;
The full tide of the swelling heart shrink dwindled to a
    thread,
The thought that burns for utterance turn to madness on
    the lips ;
And dying none shall pity, no nor mourn for him when
    dead.

ÆSCHYLUS.

How changed he is, and pale ! how colourless
His parted lips ! the eyelids yet are closed
Upon their sheathèd lightnings—all his face
Channell'd with time or tears ; those locks, that were
Like sunbeams saddened in dark water, now
White as in helpless age !—Why doth he start,
Clenching both hands, and gaze so fearfully
On vacant air ?

ORTHAGORAS.

Hush ! 'tis an awful place :
Keep silence, and regard him, for methinks
He sees some presence that we cannot see.

1st *Fury.*

Doth he now breathe and feel ? or is the blood
In his dull veins yet stagnant, and the spirit
Fast-lock'd in stony-eyed forgetfulness ?

2nd *Fury.*

We have o'er-chased our quarry : in such deep swoon
The soul finds cover, and, safe 'twixt life and death,
Makes void our effort and mocks at our revenge.

3rd *Fury.*

The lamp of sense rekindling burns so faint
As for a puff to quench : till it revive,
Seek we elsewhere a task more profitable.

1st *Fury.*

Sisters, I scent a banquet of new blood
Blown hither from the wan Sicilian fields,
Dear home of fire-eyed Havoc.   Hie we hence
Fast, fast, upon the hurricane's dark wing,
To hunt the victim down ! a tyrant there
Wades in the blood of his offenceless slaves,
And revels in their groans : crack, snaky whips,
And lash him into madness!   We'll be there
Before the axe now lifted has cut through
The cowering victim's throat : then, hither back
Returning, we may mend this broken task,
And glut our hunger in Timoleon's pain.

2nd *Fury.*

First call some torturing shape to visit him
In our enforcèd absence.

3rd *Fury.*

   'Tis well thought on :
We must not leave him idle.   Hence ! away !

       [*They vanish.*

ÆSCHYLUS.

The sky grows brighter now ; we seem to breathe
More freely : 'tis as though some stifling weight
Of thunder brooding in a sulphurous cloud
At once were lifted from the upbounding air.

ORTHAGORAS.

His eyes are open, but he sees us not :
Some spell enchains them—he is going to speak !

[Enter the Curse of DEMARISTE.

TIMOLEON.

Those fearful ones are vanish'd : what art thou ?

The Curse.

I am the embodied curse once pass'd on thee
By her that was thy mother ; and I am charged
On earth and under it, through life and death,
To cleave and fasten to thy guilty side
For ever.

TIMOLEON.

Thou art a lying phantom call'd
And conjured by the fiends that fashion'd thee
From hell, where they inhabit.   If thou hast power
To blast me, speak again those awful words,
That still are burnt upon my memory ; speak,
And I will tremble.   No, it vanishes !

[Exit Curse.

But what new horror rises on my sight ?

[Enter the Ghost of TIMOPHANES.

Can the impalpable void womb of air
Breed spectres at your will, and people space
With shadowy semblances of forms that were ?

See! see! Timophanes! in garb and mien
As when he met us on that fateful morn
Beneath the citadel!   Unhappy soul!
If such thou art, I charge thee lay aside
That shape which is the token of thy sin
And mine undoing: with those blood-stained hands,
Hot cruel eyes, and crown-polluted brow,
Thou canst not even move me to regret.

[Exit Ghost.

This was no offspring of a fever'd brain:
It made as though 'twould speak, when suddenly
A thrill of trembling seized its vapoury form,
And, as pursued by some o'ermastering fear,
Eyes all averted, and without a word,
It vanish'd as it came!

ÆSCHYLUS.

His face is sad,
But has resumed its wonted majesty,
No longer horror-stricken.

ORTHAGORAS.

Nay, he smiles,
As to some loved one hov'ring o'er him.

[Enter the Spirit of Liberty.

TIMOLEON.

Ah ! who is this with locks uncrown'd and lips unkiss'd
    of kings ?
Who is this Spirit, hither speeds with light upon her
    wings ?
Love's rapture in her fearless eyes, from far she tra-
    velleth,
As one who wist not of a world made desolate with
    death.

The Spirit of Liberty.

My temple is not on the earth ; I roam through air and
    sea ;
A wanderer and without a land, my name is Liberty :
Men hunt me from the homes I bless ; they desecrate
    my shrine ;
But I come to thee, O well-belov'd, to claim and call
    thee mine.

TIMOLEON.

Alas ! that thou should'st call in vain ! Thou speakest
    to a slave
Whose chains are strong as adamant, whose dungeon as
    the grave.
My soul is crush'd beneath a curse, and who shall set
    me free ?
I may not cast my burden down, nor rise and follow
    thee.

The Spirit of Liberty.

Thou wert not wont to fold thine arms, nor fain to hang
the head ;

When warriors waited on thy lips, not such the words
they said ;

Nor had ten thousand curses tamed the heart so cowed
and cold

Toward her who once thy worship was, who loved thee
from of old.

TIMOLEON.

Ah ! chide not, for thou dost not know the change of
time and fate,

The fire that fell, the sword that slew, her love which
turned to hate ;

There is no balm to heal, no word of solace to be said :

Would God she had travailèd ere her time, and died,
and borne me dead !

The Spirit of Liberty.

Have I not grieved in all thy grief ? not wept thy woes
to see ?

My child, even mine, my youngest-born, what help have
I but thee ?

What need but for their sorrow's sake who battle still
with wrong ?

For they that strike for Liberty must toil and tarry long.

TIMOLEON.

O cast thine arms about my neck ! O teach my limbs to
stand !

I cannot sleep but in thine arms, nor walk but with thy
hand ;

O my new mother ! I am fain thy new-born son to be ;

But who shall break the bands of hell, that hold me still
from thee ?

The Spirit of Liberty.

I touch thee with my gentle wand ; I call thee by thy
name :

Timoleon ! rise ; thy fetters fall ; thy fears are put to
shame ;

My priest and champion thou shalt be ; and I to guard
and guide

Am still, though hidden from thy sight, for ever at thy
side.

[*She vanishes.*

ÆSCHYLUS.

See, now he rises ! and the old battle-light
Burns on his features !   'Tis as when some rock
Out-frowns a tempest, that has all day long
Rolled up the thunder of ten thousand waves,
And boomed against his bases, but at eve,
Flush'd with disastrous sunset, grimly smiles
Defiance to the untamed and treacherous sea.

5 *

ORTHAGORAS.

Let us go forward and unfold to him
The purport of our coming; in his eyes
I read glad welcome, and a joyful ' yes '
To Corinth's high commission.

> [*They advance towards him.*

TIMOLEON.

O my friends !
With what auspicious omen hath this hour
Leapt from the lap of time to comfort me
With your sweet presence !   Do you know me still,
Changed as I am, and love me? years and grief,
That wrought this ruin on my frame, have made
No havoc of my heart : give me your hands—
Nay, both together ; since I clasped them thus,
I tell you I have made such inward proof
Of sorrow's fierce caresses, I have served
A term so bitter at her sobering craft,
That till this moment, with rare interval
And seldom respite, had my dearest friend
Brought me vast tidings of invasion quelled,
Or mighty armies mustering to o'erthrow
Some slaughter-house of tyrants, and set up
A fallen freedom, I should scarce have heard,
Much less made answer or regarded him.

Nay, ye had found me one brief hour agone
Feast-master sitting at no cheerful board,
The unwilling host of such strange visitors
As might have marred your welcome.   But rejoice,
For now the gods have sent you as a sign,
That these are foiled for ever.

ORTHAGORAS.

Every word
Thou utterest, like sweet sunshine, turns some flower
Of hope to ripeness of fulfilled desire.

ÆSCHYLUS.

I never looked to see such happiness,
Or hear these comfortable words from thee.

TIMOLEON.

Come rest we on yon bank ; the shadows there
Are coolest ; you have travelled far afoot,
And must be hot and weary with the way.

ÆSCHYLUS.

Nay, for the bearer of good news or ill
Runs swiftly, and his feet forget to tire.

TIMOLEON.

Pray you, what news ?   I am as one long dead
Raised up to hear it.   Tell me by degrees
From the beginning, nowise suddenly.

ÆSCHYLUS.

'Tis old old news, too common to be new,
Nor like to startle thine accustomed ear ;
It needs no sheltering avenues of speech
To preface in these days dark deeds of blood,
And piteous cries for succour.

TIMOLEON.

Ah ! say on.

ÆSCHYLUS.

Thou knowest that Dionysius reigns again
Two years in Syracuse.

TIMOLEON.

I knew it not,
But deemed that since Callippus, he who slew
Dion, had perished by the selfsame sword,
The State, now sceptreless and made a prey
To general rapine and fierce rival feuds,
Lay festering in a swamp of anarchy.

ÆSCHYLUS.

So for six years it miserably endured,
When, as foul insects on a poor maimed beast
Fasten and feed, and swarm about its sore,
Draining the life-blood, till to make an end
Down swoops some famished vulture—so these men,

Lewd parasites and lawless mercenaries,
Robbed, hacked, and pilled, till half the strength was
    sucked
From out poor Sicily, when she and they
Together, torn and quivering in the clutch,
Became one morsel for his ravenous maw.
    Then waxed yet grosser his insatiate greed,
And from the coals of never-quenched desire,
Fanned by this gust of fortune, leapt a flame
So bloody that beside its baleful light
The torch-fire of each lesser tyranny
Shrunk into darkness.   Corinth heard and mourned
The voice of her child's anguish ; for a sound
Confused and frightful, echoes of deep groans,
And savage laughter, and imploring shrieks,
Mingled with ocean's uproar, and went forth
Among the nations.   But the third day since
Came tidings of clear colour, and withal
This message of entreaty—"Syracuse,
Down-trod by tyrants even to the dust,
To Corinth her own mother cries for aid,
And vengeance on the oppressor."   He that spake
Made all hearts sick with horror, all eyes wet
For pity, as, diving in deep gulfs of sin,
With nets of silk-meshed utterance he drew forth
The abominations of that foul abyss.

Yea, and some doubted of the things they heard,
So monstrous grew the tale, as was unrolled
The crimeful record of his rank excess—
His catlike cunning and mad tiger-thirst
For bloodshed, his luxurious appetite,
In brutish instinct and ungoverned lust
Out-grovelling all before him.   Furthermore
To make despair more desperate, even to blight
The opening bud of young rebellion,
Like a dark living cloud upon their shores,
Dread foes to freedom and fair Sicily,
The Punic hosts were gathering.   To be brief,
This woeful chronicle and sad appeal
So moved the heart of Corinth, that next morn
Before the assembled State's high majesty,
The people with one shout consenting cried
To send the wished-for succour.

TIMOLEON.

That was well :
Whom chose they to command and marshal them ?

ÆSCHYLUS.

That question probes a wound thyself must heal,
Or perish Syracuse ! for when the shout
Ceased, and the Archons to the crowd set forth
Some leader for their choice, each hero named

Forbad them, and no captain of them all
In such a cause, so hopeless, against such odds,
Durst gird him to the danger.   Then was heard
A voice, from whence I know not, no man knew,
Which 'mid the silence like a trumpet rang
And cried 'Timoleon!' and with such a roar
As though the elements of air and sea
Commingling in one crash made sudden league
To ravage and o'erride the continent,
So from that multitude of tongues poured forth
An inundation of tempestuous sound,
That broke in thunder, as they caught the cry,
And tossed it to the clouds—'Timoleon!'

TIMOLEON (*after a pause*).

This is the last time I shall watch the sun
Go down behind Cyllene to the sea,
And flood these fields with splendour, which I loved,
Despite of all my suffering.   Let us rise:
How calm it is and cool! and how the breeze
Fills with contagious freedom all my soul!
Enter, my friends, for ye have fasted long
Since morn; and thou, Orthagoras, presently
Do sacrifice for us; I think indeed
The gods are favourable, and have heard my prayer,
And I am fain to worship.

ORTHAGORAS.

'Tis most meet
We pay these solemn rites, and then to rest;
For ere to-morrow from the Ægean wave
Flush the proud forehead of the citadel,
We should be gone.

ÆSCHYLUS.

Set we not forth to-night?

TIMOLEON.

To-night.

So, false ones, ye are foiled at last,
And the sweet vision triumphs, and is true!

ACT II.

SCENE II.—*The Market-place in Corinth.*

[*Enter Citizens.*

1st Citizen.

NEIGHBOUR, good speed!   Whence come you?

2nd Citizen.

From Lechæum.

1st Citizen.

Is aught there rumoured of the expedition?

2nd Citizen.

The air is rife with floating hearsay tales
Of such diverse complexions as to match
The tints and tissues of men's hopes and fears—
Frail threads by each from native fancy spun,
And dyed with his heart's colour.   In one morn
I have heard news should make one drunk with tears,
And mad with exultation: first, our ships
Are sunk or taken, and Timoleon slain;
Next, by a storm they're scattered; now, 'tis sure

The Carthaginian fleet holds all the strait,
And lets them from the passage ; and, once more,
These have been wonderfully put to flight,
And Syracuse delivered, in less time
Than had sufficed the speed of Argo's prow
To dance us back the tidings.

1st Citizen.

                        Holds that news
Of the Leontine tyrant, Hiketas ?
'Tis said he hath joined Carthage, and broke off
Our friendship on some hollow vain pretence.

2nd Citizen.

Yea, shall the oppressor strike for liberty?
Or shall a snake's lip kiss thee, and not sting ?
His mouth dropped sweetness, that fond Syracuse
Might suck the sugared venom, and himself
Devouring the vile pest she groans beneath,
And greeted as deliverer, might therewith
Be taken to her heart and so strike home.

Countryman.

Ha ! therefore crew this cock his challenge-note
So loudly, and clapped wings till all the roost
'Gan wonder, that himself anon might strut
The Dionysian dunghill !

1st Citizen.

'Tis a quest
Of wild adventure and nigh desperate hope,
Timoleon is embarked on.

Countryman.

Well, I know not ;
Such fair occasion is a savoury mess
For your king-killer, but withal served up
Too hot for the eating : little blame, say I,
Our generals feared to scald their hands in it.

1st Citizen.

Against such odds 'twill be a miracle
If e'er they dint the sands of Sicily ;
So may the gods befriend them !

Woman.

Yea, 'tis like
All gods will aid the murderer of his kin,
And cursed by his own mother, or give strength
Of battle to the hands that strike with his.

2nd Citizen.

Good dame, bethink thee ; were the deed undone,
Which thou reprov'st so sharply, Corinth now
Were even as Syracuse, and all we here
Either sad exiles, or mewed up in chains

To serve a master's pleasure—yea, thyself,
Free mother of a freeman's sons no more,
From thy slave's bosom giving suck to slaves.

1st Citizen.

Women are mothers first, then citizens.

Woman.

And men turn monsters, being citizens.   .
What ! was there none to pull the despot down,
But—heaven defend us from such citizens !—
A man must knife his brother?   I tell you still,
The high gods will avenge it, both on him
And us and on all Corinth ; for by that stain
We and the cause we fight for are accursed.
And so farewell, fair citizens.   [*Exit.*

Countryman.

Good lack !
She lows so loudly for a neighbour's calf,
Pray heaven her own 'scape slaughtering, or methinks
Her horns will clear a passage.   Were I lord
Timoleon, in good sooth I'd rather meet
Whole hosts of tyrants than a fly-stung herd
Of gadding wives.

1st Citizen.

Soft-hearted is sharp-tongued :
But men think deep what women talk abroad.

Sirs, wot you well, the general voice is now
Timoleon's, and, let victory light on him,
His only, and for ever ; but if he fail,
There are who hold 'twere better he should rot
In Syracusan dungeons, than come home
To face his friends in Corinth.

2nd Citizen.

Thou sayest well :
For dogs are dogs, and to be torn of beasts
No cleanly death ; but 'twere the viler fate,
If choice were given, to be devoured of those
One's hand has saved and fostered.

[*Enter a Soothsayer.*

Soothsayer.

Masters all,
What moody business sets your brows afrown ?
Out on such ominous eyes ! this is a time
Of joyful expectation.

2nd Citizen.

By thy looks
Thou art of those who from strange mysteries
Of earth and heaven, or in the heart of beasts,
Can pluck divine foreknowledge, and by the light
Of an enthusiast mind have power to read
Dark regions of the unexplored ' to be.'

What therefore we may hear and thou canst tell,
Whether foreboding of our hopes or fears,
Delay not to unfold.

Soothsayer.

I can but speak
What all the world has heard, though some have scoffed,
Deeming them idle tales, how that the gods,
By solemn portents and peculiar signs,
Unequalled in our age, surpassed in none,
Vouchsafed to smile on our departing arms,
And shower their favours on Timoleon.

2nd Citizen.

Something we heard—no constant clear report,
But such vague rumour as, from mouth to mouth
Bandied, and buzzed into the credulous ear·
Of idle multitudes, breeds monstrous forms,
Ten thousand in a moment: but if aught
Thou holdst for certain, or thyself hast seen,
Say on, thou shalt have eager audience.

Countryman.

Ay, speak ; I warrant 'tis a wondrous tale.

Soothsayer.

Know then, ere yet our musters were equipped,
While Corinth rang with warlike gathering,

Timoleon to the sacred Delphic shrine
Made pilgrimage ; nor ever entered there
Within the secret of its dim recess
A head more holy, a heart more reverent,
Of each due ordinance and solemn rite
A more devout observer.   As wont is,
After prayer said and sacrifices done,
His feet drew nigh that ancient chasm profound
Fast by the earth's firm centre, whence exhaled,
The ascending vapour impregnates the brain
Of the throned priestess, till her frantic lips
In riddles hard of labyrinthine speech
Utter the gods' oracular response.
Thither he came, the dread prophetic voice
Attending, in that shrine whose awful air
Simmers with secrets from the eternal deep,
If haply its dark bosom might illume,
As thunder-clouds flash on the murk of night,
The far-off issue of his great emprise.
But as he stooped to enter, and bowed down
Prostrate in adoration, lo ! a wreath
Of conquest, broidered with triumphal crowns
And images of victory, from the wall
Down-fluttering fell, and, 'lighting as he rose,
Circled the breadth of his heroic brow.

6

Countryman.

I never heard the like !

2nd Citizen.

Such signs as these
Portend momentous issues, do they not?
And greatness, and a man beloved of heaven ?

Soothsayer.

Ay, if the sacred art diviners use
Err not, and heaven be true.   But have ye heard
That dream the priestess of Persephone
Dreamed ere they put to sea?   For as she slept,
In the first watch when slumber is most deep,
Lo ! at her side the goddess ! a pale form
Shrouded in shadowy mist, whose floating folds
Caught glory from the moonlight !   There she stood
Silent, one hand upon her brow, and one
Pointing to seaward ; and she fixed on her
The yearning of those eyes whose rapt regard
Rules Erebus, remembering Sicily.
Then in no earthly accent, with like voice
To subterranean thunder she began—
"I am Persephone, that have uprisen
From the dread couch of Dis, and for awhile
Resigned my seat of gloomy sovereignty,
To visit the bright fields I loved on earth,
To visit and avenge them.   Lo ! to-night

Over the pearl path that the moonbeams make,
A twofold godhead with your fleet shall glide,
Demeter and Persephone : we will give
Clear tokens of our presence ; and doubt not
P. : in all conflicts we will guard the head
And nerve the hand that strikes for Sicily."

    So spake she, nor withheld the promised sign ;
For at the dead and darkest of the night
With freshening breeze our ships stood out to sea
Past Elis and Zakynthus, when behold !
The heavens were rent asunder, and bright flame
Shot from the zenith down, a meteor-sheaf
Of splendours, that took shape, and streamed and spread,
And in the semblance of a sacred torch
Blazed high above them on toward Italy.

2nd Citizen.

Whence learned ye this great wonder ?

Soothsayer.

From the lips

Of certain islanders—a coasting-crew—
Leucadians, who thus far upon their way
Convoyed them, and returned to tell the tale.

1st Citizen.

Are ye so sure it burned not angerly,
Charged hot with baleful menace, for a sign
Terrific, not triumphant ?

6 *

Soothsayer.

Hear that shout !

2nd Citizen.

What is't they cry?   Corinth ! Timoleon !
Some stirring news is toward!   I see a crowd
Panting and straining in the hopeless track
Of a swift runner who is hard at hand.

[*Enter a Herald.*

All.

What tidings, herald, of Timoleon ?

Herald.

For them that love him not bad news enow.

Soothsayer.

The gods be thanked !

1st Citizen.

Nay, boast not till ye know.
Marked you the phrase ? no word of Corinth yet ;
Good news belike for them that love not her.

2nd Citizen.

Nay, for this message is indeed the breath
And very heart-beat of my hope ; but thou—

Countryman.

Wast born to croak in Syracusan fens,
Foul skies or fine.   Come, honest messenger,
Give, an breath serve, a sample of thy news.

Herald.

For all your jars, good hap from first to last,
Luck and fair deeds and favourable gods
My tidings tell.   In brief, our General hath,
Despite all disadvantage—time, and place,
Cross currents of opposing circumstance,
And treacherous friendship, and designing foe—
Ay, worse than all, grazed by the rankling tooth
Of sidelong hate and harsh opinion—
Though matched with all these odds, hath none the less
From fortune's bough plucked off the topmost wreath.
And first, arrived at Rhegium, we were hailed
By Carthaginian envoys with cold words
From Hiketas—" His arms had ta'en the town,
Franked up the tyrant in his citadel,
And well-nigh ended at one stroke the war.
Our ships, no longer serviceable, might,
Nay must, all shadow of offence apart,
Sail homeward "—which to enforce, a Punic fleet
Of twice our strength lay ready.   Timoleon heard,
Feigning a forced content: nor urged he aught,
Save that in public they set forth the terms
Before the Rhegian elders.   Hereupon
The assembly met ; the city-gates were barred ;
And thus, with Rhegium's eloquence to aid,
Whose mimic zeal still fanned the mock debate,

Outwitting once the sly Phœnician,
We seized the hour, stole forth, and one by one,
Timoleon last, the more to cloak his wile,
Regained our ships, and so to Sicily.

There entertained us Tauromenium's lord,
Andromachus ; whence, after two days' rest,
On to Adranum by forced march till night ;
For faction there waxed clamorous, and men stood
Half for Timoleon, half for Hiketas.
Nine hours we toiled afoot ; the fierce sun smote
Sore on our armèd heads till darkness fell ;
Then onward still through darkness ! but at length,
Some score of furlongs from the town, our van
Halted, beholding in the plain far off
Torch-lights and bivouac-fires, and on the wind
Hearing the hum and murmur of a host,
That 'mid the tumult of encampment keeps
Slack ward, and recks not of a coming foe.

Here those that led took counsel, and the most
Bade halt till morning, and repose our strengths,
Faint with long fast and travel : but the chief
Cried out, " On ! on ! One brave brief effort more
Flings you with tenfold vantage on a foe
To-morrow thrice your power, to-night your prey
Cumbered with half-pitched tents, amid their stuff
Caught unawares and feasting." With that word

He seized his buckler, and strode on before,
Nor durst a man gainsay him : but as he spake
So it befell ; for ere the moon was risen,
With a great shout we burst upon their flank,
Down-bearing all before us : fast they fled—
As from Parnassus the sonorous north
Shrieks down the mountain hollows to break with power
On Delphi, and takes her forests by the hair,
And drives the leaves in a whirlwind—so sped they,
Swept with a sudden horror of shadowy forms
From forth the howling darkness, the strewn ranks
Of Hiketas : some we surprised in sleep,
Their last, some feasting, all of war's alarm
Secure and heedless ; so the camp, the town,
Great store of captives, and much spoil was ours.

2nd Citizen.

Where be the tongues of his accusers now ?
As mute in mouth as safe in sheath the swords
They lacked the heart to draw.   'Tis the best news
Our age hath heard.

Herald.

A better crowns that best ;
For at the point of onset, when our shout
First slew the silence, lo ! the temple-doors
Oped of the god Adranus, and his spear

Quivered in all its length, and drops of sweat
Started and trickled from its stony pores
Down to the pavement, while stark horror seized
The priestess wondering what these things should mean.
But, after, no man doubted (for his name
'Gan to be noised more loudly, and what signs
Had erst foretold him famous) that hereby
The god gave token of his grace, and hailed
Timoleon as deliverer.   From that day
The terror of his arm filled Sicily,
That many sought our friendship, chief of these
Mamercus, lord of Catana, beside
A score of lesser townships : but the top
And pinnacle of fortune's yet to tell ;
For Dionysius in the Ortygian hold
Shut fast, and now nigh hopeless to unbind
The girdle of his threefold enemy,
Corinthian, Carthaginian, Leontine,
Heard of Adranum's victory, and sent,
Scorning the yoke of conquered Hiketas,
An embassage to meet us, there and then
Surrendering unsolicited himself,
Treasure and fortress, arms and equipage
Into Timoleon's hand : nor asked he more
Than transport safe to Corinth, there to live
Henceforth unchallenged of his liberty.

2nd Citizen.

Which proffered terms were taken ?

Herald.

Ere I loosed
From shore, four hundred veterans of our host
Watched from Ortygia's bastion, having stole
Safe through the leaguer's lines ; and he whose wrath
Was like a volcano kindled, and whose breath
Blew deadlier from his nostrils than the blast
Of pestilence on Syracuse, even he,
This monster-despot in one hour become
A sign for lips to shoot at, and a mark
For Folly's outthrust finger, shall be seen
Walking in Corinth's streets, weak, poor, despised,
Unkinged, and no man trembling at his frown.

1st Citizen.

These are great tidings, herald, but methinks,
Though praise still weds the prosperous, rightly judged,
More due to feats of fortune than of war ;
Yet time may mend that verdict : howsoe'er,
It boots not him to triumph, who through some trick
And slippery practice of his nimbler wit
Hath tried one happy fall : the worst is yet
To cope with, when fast-locked with equal grip

They tug together, and overmatched he feels
The sinewy foeman's ever-tightening strain,
And plies the shift that serves no second turn.

2nd Citizen.

Sir, sir, I like not your philosophy :
O'erwise is one with foolish.   Pray you, cease :
'Tis sage-like, doubtless, with judicial frown
And air-poised chin, on dexterous finger-tip
To weigh the world's experience—but we prate
Idly : vouchsafe us, herald, of our friends
Some further news—where lies Timoleon's power ?
Whom doth Ortygia's garrison obey ?

Herald.

Neon is captain in the Citadel
With thrice eight hundred men—the more part those
Who yielded with the despot—and there lies
Blockaded, for the Carthaginian fleet
Fills the great harbour : and the city itself,
Tycha, Neapolis, Epipolæ,
And Arcadina and all the fens are held
By Hiketas and Mago.   For the rest,
Timoleon hath led back the main array,
And tarries at Adranum, till the State
Grant him some increase of his power, for which
He prays your willing voices.

Citizens.

He shall have them ;
Yea, and hath earned them well.

1st Citizen (aside).

Ay, go your ways,
Light straw-chips blown round corners of the streets,
Till some thwart current cross ye ! shout his name,
Swear by Timoleon, sweat and die for him.
No more of fratricide ! 'tis patriot now,
Tyrannicide, deliverer!   Well, let be :
Go, help him win ! send all your succours forth ;
Be flattered, fooled ; then rid you as ye may
Of your deliverer, gaping to behold
Tyrannicide turned tyrant.

Soothsayer.

Ye do well
To laud this man, who is worthy of your loves,
Being pure and perfect-hearted, toward all men
Reproveless, and for mastery of his hand
Strong, and a mighty leader.   Let who will
Go forth with him and conquer ; for the proud
Beneath his feet are stubble, but him all gods
Prosper, and make his counsel to prevail.

ACT II.

Scene III.—*A Street in Corinth.*

Time, early morning.

Chorus.

Ho! give ear and come forth at the voice of our
        calling !
    Ho! awake ye, by slumber possessed !
Ye who dwell in the land where the water-floods falling
    Mingle murmurs from east shore and west :
                Naught appalling
We bear in our bosom to utter, who summon you forth
    from your rest.

    On the rock of your god, lo ! the sunlight is burning
        Newly risen, springing swift from the sea !
    But with brighter new birth to your sister returning,
        Long-fettered, at last to be free :
                With what yearning
Of soul have I watched, have I waited, O dawn of her
    freedom, for thee !

But, behold ! him who robed himself red with the
    slaughters
  Of sons whom her bosom had borne,
With the garment of slavery girdled her daughters,
  And with moanings from night until morn,
      Winds and waters
Waft safe to his uttermost refuge of anguish and exile
    and scorn !

With the seed of the serpent from of old she had
    striven ;
  In the folds of his might she had lain ;
And she cried to the earth, but no answer was given,
  Nor none succoured her calling in vain,
      Till from heaven
Fell a bolt that was born of a woman, and slew it, and
    behold it was slain !

Not with pomp on his path, not with triumph or
    treasures,
  Not with victims to torture or slay,
Not with singing of songs or with treading of measures,
  Shall a king come to Corinth to-day :
      All the pleasures,
The lusts and fruition of kingship, are past and are
    perished for aye.

With the joy of the lyre dies the light of the jewel;
  All the garlands lie withered and stark:
But the hate is still strong in the heart of the cruel,
  Though the house of his feasting be dark:
    Yea for fuel
It shall pierce through body and spirit, and burn to the
  uttermost spark.

And the fox from the north laying wait for the
  plunder,
  And the lion-cub ready to rend,
Let them flee upon ships o'er the sea-waves that
  sunder,
  Ere they fall by the swords that defend,
    Ere they founder
Thrust down to the depths of the ocean, and brought to
  a terrible end.

For in dreams I beheld, and one rose to deliver;
  Round his loins was for girdle a chain;
And the voice of his mouth made the mountains to
  quiver,
  At the sound thereof armies were slain;
    And a river
Ran deep from the storm of the battle, and red with an
  ominous rain.

Yea, the cruel shall cease; their foundation shall
    crumble;
  From of old 'twas revealed to the wise;
They that stablish their throne on the necks of the
    humble,
  Drunk with vanity, feasted with lies,
      When they stumble,
The staff of their pride shall not aid them; they are
    fallen; they shall not arise.

  O fair city of freemen, by tyrant untaken,
    Resting safe 'neath the rock of thy might,
  Lift thy voice! for thy sister, even she the forsaken,
    Long captive, left sighing for the light,
      Doth awaken
To more than the day's reappearing, and from shades
    that were darker than night.

Corinthian Woman.

O beloved! my heart throbs for wonder:
  What is this? what new theme that ye sing?

Chorus.

'Tis of chains that are broken in sunder,
  Which we cast round the neck of a king.

Corinthian Woman.

Nay, what jubilant strains for sad ditties?
  What smiles for old tears that ye shed?

Chorus.

'Tis for Syracuse, saddest of cities,
　Rearisen from the gates of the dead.

Corinthian Woman.

Are ye wanton that mock at your sorrow,
　Ere the tide of its anguish be turned?

Chorus.

In the east marked ye not the new morrow?
　Looking westward was naught ye discerned?

Corinthian Woman.

How should dawn melt the mist of my doubting?
　How should Hope set her sign in the sky?

Chorus.

By the voices of them that are shouting,
　Lo! the hour of deliverance is nigh!

ACT II.

SCENE IV.—*The Market-place in Corinth.*

Time, a few hours later.

Stranger.

I TAKE my stand here by the oyster-stall.

Citizen.

And I with you ; 'tis excellently chosen :
The main crowd surges toward us, and behind,
Those narrowing streets will check them, and the stream
Of adverse comers.   Howsoe'er it fall,
Needs must the wealth and jetsam of the tide
Drift hither and be stranded.

Stranger.

              Well, stand firm !
By Heracles ! that child were best abed ;
They'll trample it to death !   Softly, I say ;
So, lift him o'er the shoulders.   Where 's its mother ?
Woman, what scenes are these for wide-eyes here
To be abroad in ?   Let him stand by me
Upon the bench.

Woman.

There, there, the gods forgive me !
A father, sir, yourself—I'll warrant ye.
But who'ld ha' judged sane folk would jostle so
To stare at a mere monster ?

Stranger.

That's the lure :
Look you, I live my life some threescore year,
Kind, temperate, honest, of a good report,
And none so curious casts a glance at me.
But let me rob my father, boil my child,
Or carve my wife to collops—from that hour
'Twill cost you a bruised foot and aching ribs
To meet me in the market.

Citizen.

Hist ! I say :
Read no more lectures, friend philosopher,
Or have Diogenes for auditory.

Stranger.
Him of Sinope?

Citizen.

Just in front : you see
The slouching shoulders ? there ! his face half turns—

Skin lava-colour like a dead volcano—
Cross under-lip—its fellow warping back
Cuts furrows in the cheek.   Pray notice him.

Stranger.

It is a sour and frost-pinched countenance.

Citizen.

Yet, should he shift full front, beneath that bush
There burns an eye, you'ld haply feel the glance of,
Ay, and the man behind you.

Stranger.

                    We're in luck.

Is't likely he'll accost him?

Citizen.

                    Time will show.

Look ! there 's a stir to leftward ! yon black wave
Should vomit forth some wonder—How it boils !
Now then on tip-toe ! that must be the man !

[*Enter* DIONYSIUS, *with the crowd.*

DIONYSIUS.

Friends, I come hither not upon compulsion,
But in assured regard of your fair faiths,
With a whole skin and with a mind to keep it,
Not to be pulled, so please you, limb from limb

7 *

Piecemeal—a service which Timoleon's pikes
With cleanlier, more convenient despatch
Had rendered for the asking.

Citizen.

'Twas a boon,
I wonder was not offered out of hand.

Stranger.

Mayhap your General searched his memory,
And called to mind an old deliverance wrought—
A certain tyrant slain upon a time—
And how ye dealt with the deliverer;
Thinking 'not twice shall they cry out on blood;
Their pity shall live with them.'

Dionysius.

Oh! these knaves!
'Tis a flesh-mountain! nay, a chain of them
Piled each on other!   Here's a mother's son
Outgaping Ætna for Empedocles!
Sir—you're a soldier—use your privilege
Of oath and thrust to clear some halberd-space
For lungs to breathe by; or your poor sport in me
Were like to end with what 'twould feed upon.

[A space is cleared.

I thank you, friends ; your welcome is so warm,
It robs me of my breath.   Forgive me, sirs,
If till this moment some ill-masked surprise
At the profuseness of your courtesy—
Our island-manner lacks abandonment—
Mixed with the feelings of a fallen man,
Withheld me somewhat from your kind embraces,
Which no less nearly touch me, that the joy
Of their supportment jeopardies my life.
Believe me, ne'er on Syracusan soil
Did such fair numbers press to wait on me.

A Merchant.

I have heard say you were too prodigal,
Too thoughtless-lavish of your subjects' lives :
True they were bondsmen and a barren breed ;
But things worth having are worth husbanding,
And for much traffic in the murderer's trade
Thrift is a virtue that commends itself.

Dionysius.

Your free Corinthian censure sticks and stings ;
Our courts breed none so thorny : but alas !
Good counsel comes belated ; yet methinks
' Live and let live ' may be the people's cry,
But with a tyrant 'tis ' let live and die.'

A Voice.

Down with the monster!

A Bystander.

               Nay, what's left of him
Can down no deeper; 'tis an upward step
From life's worst thrall to death's enfranchisement.

Voice.

What bondage holds the tyrant while he breathes?

Bystander.

A threefold fetter of lust, fear, and shame.

A Second Voice.

Why, then, forbear and lay no hands on him;
Wouldst raise him to the rank of honest corpse?

A Third Voice.

Rank enough then, I'se warrant!

DIOGENES.

               Fishmonger,
Have you no purple-fish for majesty?

Fishmonger.

Here are good oysters, an it please your wisdom.

Soldier.

And here's a sword-fish, he's right welcome to,
Fresh from the cutler—draws rare purple-dye.

DIOGENES.

Give me an oyster, fellow; I would read.

Third Voice.

Read from an oyster?

A Fourth Voice.

Ay, an it be open.

DIOGENES (*opening oyster*).

States are like oysters : this rough outer wall,
Or sheltering casket, is the Constitution,
Framed to protect the floating life within,
Our Body Politic, which left naked else
To prowling neighbours or anarchic storms,
Being so volatile and watery-weak,
Must perish in the great sea-wildernesses.
Thus far thrive all : but silently there forms
Upon the polished concave an opaque
Yet shining drop, that hardens to the shell—
A taint, a tumour—'tyranny' we'll call it :
And fungus-like this fair deformity
Usurps the vital office all for show,
Starves what it lives by, and luxuriates
Upon the general leanness, till at length,
All powers of life exhausted, there remains
The cold dead splendour of a heartless pearl.

DIONYSIUS.

More eloquent than just: sir, give me leave
To patch your fancy-fine comparison
With some poor rags of old experience.
This fair disease, which fastens to the shell
Of the sick fish, bred ever from within,
And waxing ever an insatiate sore,
I liken to the lust of liberty,
Who sits white-throned upon the market-places,
Drinking the blood of them that serve her best.
Then drops the diver godlike from above—
Your tyrant, mark you—to the dim sea-depth
Plunging, lifts oyster to the upper air,
Slits casket open, feasts upon his find,
Putting what else were useless to fair use,
And plucks me forth your pearl of liberty
To shine upon his finger.

Third Voice.

Great Hephæstus !

This fellow lacks not mettle.

Fourth Voice.

Nay, 'tis ever

Your brazen forehead fits the golden crown.

DIONYSIUS.

'Tis easy for you thus to jeer at me :
Ye are the stronger, and I needs must yield :

And yet methinks—your patience for a while—
'Twere not so hard, if balance should be struck,
And from the offending scale all odds removed,
As weight of birth and bent of circumstance,
In the main trespass of my grave offence
To prove you guilty in a near degree.
All men, I think, love power ; then why not I ?
Is wealth to all men precious ? then to me ;
Beauty and wit and mirth and adulation
Even a mean man may despise from far ;
But being present they appear so sweet
As hardly shall the wisest part from them.
I will be frank, I follow mine own lust ;
So do not ye the same ?—I tyrannized ;
Are ye not tyrants, now at least, to me ?
Thou cynic-censor, have with thee I say
For a right comrade of mine ancient craft,
Nay master, ere my prenticehood began !
For prithee since what hour of yesterday
Hast thou not absolutely set thy yoke
Upon the weaker, or that rod, thy mouth,
Lash'd with the terrors of sharp-wounding words,
Not pitilessly wielded?   Yea, thou art
More peremptory with thy cloudy brows
To o'ercast pleasure, and turn smiles to frowns
And mirth to sadness, than the inexorable

And despot darkness of a winter's night.
Dost thou not sit within thy palace-tub
Sending a thousand gloomy couriers forth—
Sour looks and sullen thoughts and humorous spleen—
Thine arbitrary instruments, to kill
All rebel joys, that band them in revolt
Against thy vile usurped authority?

Citizen.

See how his heart brims o'er with holy zeal,
Moistening his eyelid with a virtuous tear !

DIOGENES.

An tears from such a droughty source should fall,
Be Afric's desert henceforth full of springs,
And rain-showers from clear skies no prodigy.

DIONYSIUS.

Hadst thou the substance of the thing thou claim'st,
The sovereign eye, the soul's pre-eminence,
To sway the passions, awe the thoughts of men,
Out-shouldering now the base and pigmy crowd
That flouts the brokeng gods it bowed before,
Thou hadst been what thou art not, great enough
Of thine abundant grace to pity me.

DIOGENES.

Pity thee, I ! thou spot ! thou sepulchre !—
Wert thou not meaner than the least and lowest

Of all the thousands thou hast soiled or slain,
Or if wrong-doing and suffering weighed as one
To purchase this pure medicine of the soul,
This pity, and didst thou claim it for that thou
Art what thou art, not other than thou wert,
Then wert thou pitiable, and more than these,
As by thy vileness thou art wretcheder.
But now—O heavens !—because thou art clean cut off
From the foul savour of thy former sin,
In whose corrupt abominable embrace
Festering thou layest, because thou art no more tied
To a dead carcase in a stagnant fen,
But canst arise and cleanse thyself and go,
Dost thou claim pity?   Dost thou sigh for *this*
' Ah me ! the heavy change ? '   I tell thee truth,
The gods in heaven could wield no blacker bolt,
Nor man mete worthier doom, than thee to drive
Back to thine old pollution, saying, ' O swine !
What doest thou in the sheep-fold, where white sheep
Feed in fair grass, not garbage ?   Out on thee !
Back to thy slush, and wallow ! '
                              As for these
And me, the judgment of thy slanderous tongue,
To thine own damning, thus far craves response,
Because thou hast taken a thin weak thread of truth,
And twisted it with lies about, to bear

A weight which singly 'twould have snapt withal.
And first, all proper discrepance of creed
I waive, take stand upon this lower ground,
That all men aim at pleasure ; for as there yawns
Wide space in separate heavens 'twixt star and star,
Which from the vast remoteness of our earth
Do seem contiguous fires, so viewed with thee
Antisthenes and Plato shine as peers
Twinned by the huger distance.   Wherefore note,
It is not as Diogenes I speak,
' Scorn pleasure, seek the good ; ' but here and thus
Alighting off that prouder pedestal,
On your own premise I will prove you lie.

    Let pleasure therefore be the general goal :
There are more pleasures in the world than one,
Or, let me say, more semblances of her,
More lusts and more ambitions, and of these
Some that debase not, others that debase.
A man may thirst for wisdom or for wine,
May burn for knowledge or for neighbour's wife,
Aspire to serve the state or sink to enslave,
Such mere divergence widening to the gulf
"Twixt demigod and—Dionysius :
One dog-like hunts to earth his grovelling prey,
Skulks in dark corners, and devours it there,
One like a new-beaked eagle, plumèd king,

Mounts to his pastime on the morning cloud.
'Tis not that fools alone do pleasure seek,
But that the wise man knows her when he sees,
And follows not, but shuns, her counterfeit.

To thee came wisdom once with open lips
To learn thee of true pleasure : what didst thou
But cast her forth with curses from the door?
Yea, this know all, that thou the king of fools,
Turning deaf ears on Plato, didst suspect
And spurn him from thee—beast and blind !—as if
A mole should to the sheltering mountain say,
'O mountain ! though by thee all creatures live,
And though thy giant sides up-slope to heaven,
I have burrowed in thee, but have found no light;
Thou art a burden; go: I banish thee.'

DIONYSIUS.

You press too hotly, ply too cross a fence :
How might I hope your naked point to foil,
Who did but thrust for sport with blunted edge ?
Yet one pass let me parry :   Round a king
Range ever those masked faces painted ' friend,'
That live by flattery, flourish on deceit,
Gross parasites, who serve for what they suck,
No loyal service, apes of loyalty,
That brook not the shrewd searching wind of truth

To blow upon them, lest it chance to pluck
The frippery from their falseness.   How should such
Consort with Plato, sit at the same board ?
A demigod with jugglers cheek by jowl !

     Yet once I sought him, once was wholly his,
Abjured all error, loved philosophy,
And lived it, for a season : these it was
Whose clamorous hate and whispered envyings
Half forced and half beguiled me—' Lo,' said they,
' For all his lopping of thy leaves and boughs,
Digs but for Dion this wise gardener ;
And thee the crooked and earth-darkening oak,
With hollow trunk albeit, a world of shade,
He will up-root, pluck down, and plant instead
This upstart poplar, whose pinched girth shall give
Scarce foothold for a fowl to roost upon.'
So, sirs, was I seduced from my best friend.
'Tis true of all men, rulers most of all,
Our best, worst, actions are but half our own,
As when the ram goes battering, they that push
Are parcels of the weight they seem to wield,
And each partakes the engine's impetus :
When the whole body's sick, the head will swim—
' Vertigo '—'tis the common bane of kings ;
Yet 'twere fools' doctrine but to blame the head.

     Too much methinks of this: I am not here

To prop the old up, but to prove the new :
Henceforth shall no man shake me by the robe,
Nor call me tyrant ; yet look I to find
Mirth and contentment : flung from Fortune's back
I will e'en trudge it patiently afoot,
Let who will mount the runaway.   Thus far
May Plato's wisdom profit us.

DIOGENES.

Amen.

[*Exit, the crowd now dispersing.*

DIONYSIUS.

This grave discourse, it seems, has somewhat thinned
Our audience, and the streets begin to clear.
—Ho ! there's a friendly face ! Old guest of mine,
Turn host, and take me home with thee to dine.

[*Exit.*

Citizen.

Well, friend, what think you ? setting man by man,
Who showed the greatest of this company ?

Stranger.

How if I answered Dionysius ?

Citizen.

There clings an air of grandeur to the man,

That proves how mere a rag is royalty,
When such a slave can wear it.

Stranger.

           Life for life
I know of course what each of us would say ;
But should it hang upon this morning's test,
Which steel's the tougher, one alone was bent :
Wise words are easy ; but 'tis no slight proof
To spring back straightly from so sharp a strain,
And ne'er betray the pressure.

Citizen.

           Swords of lead
Do herein ape the temper of true steel,
Being bent or straightened by an infant's touch.
Look you, there go the children with their crowns
To cast on Ares' altar ! and to-night
There will be feasting toward with dance and song
Praising Timoleon and his victory :
That man, believe me, will not shun the show;
From some safe corner he'll be there to see,
Gaze on the glancing ankles, cup in hand,
And long to lead the revellers—out upon it !
One that would feast at his own funeral !
Most pliant-tempered truly !—shall we go ?

Child.

Mother !

Woman.

Now, little Timon, hand in hand,
Come, quickly !

Child.

Mother, who was that poor man ?

Woman.

One that was rich, child, cruel, and a king :
A must not pity such.

Child.

An 't be not wicked,
I hope that some one will be kind to him.

[*Exeunt.*

ACT III.

SCENE I.—*The Fens before Syracuse.*

Corinthian soldiers fishing for eels.

1st Cor. Soldier.

'TIS very merciful of the gods and Hiketas to give us such good sport.

2nd Cor. Soldier.

The gods are indeed manifestly with us; for if this same Hiketas had not been fooled by them to go gadding after Timoleon out of Acradina into Catana, and if our good captain Neon had not thereupon leapt out of Ortygia into Acradina, and if the aforesaid Hiketas had not hereupon doubled and turned back from Catana, alwithstanding he was but three parts there, and too lag to save me Acradina—

1st Cor. Soldier.

Why then thou wouldst never have talked this lumping eel into a tangle with my hook; for at the third 'if,' being choleric at thy tediousness, I whips smartly up, and there a had him fast by the belly. 'Fore Zeus, 'tis a lively fellow, and wraggles like a Carthaginian.

2nd Cor. Soldier.

How like a Carthaginian?

1st Cor. Soldier.

Thou art but a clod-poll to ask it. What! canst not by this time perceive that Mago doth suspect a taste of iron in the bait that Hiketas hath thrown him, and would fain extirpate himself, and off again to Carthage? But whereas this eel—may it perish foully—but ties itself the tighter by its kickings, our slippery friend yonder will dance himself off the barb to better purpose. I tell thee they are all sworn worshippers to the god of running away. Canst thou not prognosicate? Canst thou not smell the future?

2nd Cor. Soldier.

Nay, I was ever content with the living present, though to-morrow should be the death of me; come what will, as is like enough it may.

1st Cor. Soldier.

A shrewd answer: but certes, comrade, though thou art not learned of augury, nor hast the virtue of a reconnoitring nose, yet canst thou make shift to trust the hearing of thine own ears.

2nd Cor. Soldier.

Yea, by Pan, I will measure mine own ears with any

8 *

man's, be he man or beast; but how if thy tongue play false with mine ears, and stab them with a lying thrust, when they chance to look another way? The tongue is a long weapon and a wicked.

1st Cor. Soldier.

And if it be, are not thine ears tall enow to stand up against it, and do they not look all ways together, being moreover two to one? But see! here comes a party of our good friends the enemy: now will I broach them, and thou shalt suck wisdom—

[*Enter Greek Mercenaries of* HIKETAS.

— Welcome, worthy antagonists! Is there to be no knocking of heads together, no evacuation of the fleshly fortress for a season?

1st Mercenary.

Ay, we be suffered to rest from killing for the nonce, an it please Timoleon.

1st Cor. Soldier.

Well, 'tis a fine day, and I grudge not that thou shouldst live it out. Fishing hath not half the peril of fighting, let alone the question of them that have no quarrel, and the same flesh and blood.

2nd Mercenary.

Sir, 'tis a parlous game and very pitiful; but a soldier lives to kill, and a must needs kill to live.

1st Cor. Soldier.

Ay, but not his own neighbours, look ye. If you that serve Hiketas take up against us that are Timoleon's men, you crack our crowns to-day and your own to-morrow.

1st Mercenary.

How prove ye that, by Bacchus?

1st Cor. Soldier.

Marry, are not all we Greeks and the natural friends of Greeks?

1st Mercenary.

Yea.

1st Cor. Soldier.

Are not all Carthaginians barbarians and the natural enemies of Greeks?

1st Mercenary.

Why, yea.

1st Cor. Soldier.

Therefore are ye helping your natural enemies against your natural friends—a swift conclusion, and yet quick to come at, that even a heavy-armed foot-soldier like thyself may follow and overtake it.

1st Mercenary.

Nay, then, by the limp of the fire-god, your conclusion must be lame.   But how if our natural enemies become unnaturally our friends ?   for in good sooth we serve Hiketas, and the Carthaginians fight for us, not we for them.

1st Cor. Soldier.

I pray the gods pardon them that made thee ; since to forge so thick a pate, where there be no brains, is sheer wasting of a good skull.   Dost thou with sincerity believe that all this host swam hither from the pillars of Heracles to set up Hiketas ?

1st Mercenary.

Nay, that a cannot tell.

1st Cor. Soldier.

As like to set up thee.   Harkee, friend, when they have conquered us with your help, they will cast you off without it, as thou shalt see me serve this fishing-gear anon, for all it hath helped me to a good belly-full.

2nd Mercenary.

By Hermes, 'twere a scurvy bargain, but I've heard it whispered.

1st Cor. Soldier.

Yea, and there's worse comes after ; for verily, as our Captain saith, with those foreign rascals the word hath still been 'left foot Sicily, right foot Hellas,' and this same three-cornered island—what is it but the barbican of our own country yonder?

2nd Cor. Soldier.

Well, well, pity it were that a place made so excellent for our defence should fall into the hands of the barbarians.

2nd Mercenary.

So it were indeed, so it were.

1st Cor. Soldier.

Rather than give them Sicily, ye ought to wish there were many Sicilies 'twixt them and us.

1st Mercenary.

Marry and shall, by Artemis ; 'tis very just.

1st Cor. Soldier.

Well then, do ye digest this matter, an ye can stomach the flavour on't, and serve out the like measure to your mates : Timoleon is a kind general no less than a victorious. Farewell ; to-morrow mayhap we meet as comrades.

Mercenaries.

Very like, very like ; farewell, we thank ye for your good fellowship.

[*Exeunt Mercenaries.*

1st Cor. Soldier.

So, wag tongues and work spell, suspicion sucks hither the power of Hiketas, and scares me home the wary Mago to Carthage and crucifixion.

ACT III.

SCENE II.—*A Chamber in the Citadel of Ortygia.*

DEINARCHUS, ISIAS, DEMARETUS, NEON, *seated in council,*
await the arrival of TIMOLEON.

DEINARCHUS.

WAS ever yet such hopeless-seeming task
So fondly dared, so fortunately done ?
Corinth will not believe it.

DEMARETUS.

Yestermorn
Two mighty powers colleaguing overawed
And penned us in our suburbs : now, to-night,
One by mad panic is dispersed, and one
Driven from his fastness by our fierce assault
Leaves all the field unchallenged.

NEON.

'Twill be said
The gods, and not Timoleon, won the day.

DEINARCHUS.

Indeed the common sort do so regard him
As the elected instrument of heaven ;

He doth affect communion with the gods ;
And much portentous rumour noised abroad
Hath holp confirm them in their phantasy.

NEON.

I would ye had seen him lead the main array
This morning o'er Anapus : it were strange
But ye had shared their fond credulity.

DEMARETUS.

I and Deinarchus from Epipolæ
Were part beholders—for the northern slopes
Scarce checked our onset—how he stormed the town,
Scaling the heights to southward.

ISIAS.

                  On the east
I met but feigned resistance ; all the brunt
And heat of this day's action fell to him.

DEINARCHUS.

Methinks the foe was conquered ere we joined,
The war-heart in them numbed and frozen quite
By Mago's cold desertion.

DEMARETUS.

             In success
Lies still the crown of honour : Mago fled
As fearing Hiketas was false to him ;

For this man's fortune so turns all to gain,
His very foes appear his pensioners,
And their worst plots but masks of amity.

ISIAS.

How think ye he will use what he hath won?

DEMARETUS.

As who casts treasure to the squandering sea :
Ah ! much I fear he'll yield the gripe of power
And hard-earned harvest of our conquering arms
To the weak fingers of a scrambling mob,
Till license grow more sick than tyranny.
Ye know me, friends, no tyrant's man am I,
But flocks need shepherding, when wolves are by.

DEINARCHUS.

For our own sakes we must not suffer it :
What ! foil the wrestler, and refuse the prize !

NEON.

His conscience is so fine a colander,
'Twill ne'er sift heaps for pride to perch upon ;
The very dust of honour scarce gets through,
Much less the coarse stuff of ambition.
But see ! he comes : we shall know more anon.

[*Enter* TIMOLEON.

TIMOLEON.

Brave comrades, hail ! and Corinth's thanks to each ;
I dare anticipate her just award
For the great labours of this happy day :
So far as any man have praise herein,
It shall be shared by all indifferently ;
Our threefold venture was thrice fortunate,
Nor no man failed in aught : yet, if the palm
Of all this conflict were assigned to one,
I'd say 'tis Neon's, whose expedient zeal
Falling at vantage on the eastern ports
First gave us foothold for to-day's exploit ;
Hereto will all assent : for my part I
Abjure all merit save of duty done,
So plain I trace the handiwork of heaven :
For, first, the weight of half our enterprise
Was lifted from us with no help of ours—
We woke, and it had vanished ! now to-night,
The very topmost of our hope is scaled,
And not one slain to sigh for ! add to this
The scattered powers of conquered Hiketas
Break their allegiance, and turned back from flight
Do hourly flock to us.

NEON.

Lord General,
To one whose fame is bruited through the world

Our weak additions are a thing of course,
And needs must seem superfluous ; from the heart
Nathless we greet thy triumph.

DEINARCHUS.

But that I dread
The verdict of presumption, I would urge
That no misprisal of thy proper worth,
No self-abatement, fearing to be great,
Seduce thee from thine office, to forego
The trust which heaven itself commits to thee.

TIMOLEON.

Ye shall not find me backward ; at this hour,
When all are wearied, and night wears apace,
And every eye but ours is slumber-bound,
I ask ye hither and trespass on your rest,
To apprise you of my purpose, that hereby,
Measuring the scope and working of my mind,
Ye might not blame its suddenness : meanwhile
Ye have conjectured something of my thought—
Your faces tell the tale : 'tis briefly this :—
To-morrow morn the public criers shall go
Their circuit of the city, to proclaim
Freedom in Syracuse ; I reinstate
In the full rights of old enfranchisement
Without distinction all her citizens :

The broken fabric of the commonwealth—
That ancient model framed by Diocles—
With help of wisest State-artificers
Shall be with all expediency repaired :
Next, that I may not for one single day
Be damned in men's opinion, while they view
This time-dishonoured hold of gloomy power,
I herewithal invoke, who can, to aid
With axe and bar, who will, with mere main strength,
Its demolition, that to dust may come
The Dionysian fortress ; in its stead
A common hall for judgment shall be reared,
First need of a free people.   Furthermore,
Because the ways are desolate, and Despair
Sits gaping in the market, and rich men
Are not, but slain or banished, I invite
From all far countries the returning steps
Of exiles, whencesoe'er of Italy,
Or Hellas, or of utmost ocean-lands,
My heralds may convene them : and, lest these
Redeem not her impoverishment, that wealth
Once more may traffic in her silent streets
And fertilize her furrows, we will seek
Strange settlers to our city ; there shall gleam
White sails of foreign men from over sea,
And Corinth shall conduct them, shall with pomp

Her ancient Syracuse inaugurate
Anew, with happier omen than of old.

DEINARCHUS.

My lord, we trusted rather to have learnt
Thyself wouldst brace thee to the yoke of power ;
The ox is loosed and out, that would not draw,
But the wain stirs not, and the mire is deep.

DEMARETUS.

Sir, we have heard your hope for Syracuse ;
Such consummation is far off as yet,
Though all desire it, no man more than I.
The broken limb needs binding ere it hold,
Nor call for crutch to help the body's weight ;
One starved from childhood, penned in poisonous air,
Arrives not at man's stature, though he chance
To light on a large house with food enough.

NEON.

Yet if the vigour of new blood might be
Drawn from health's very centre, and infused
Into the sickly vessels, who'ld despair
Of renovation and organic growth ?

DEMARETUS.

Wait then : though thought o'erleap the interval,
In act 'tis vain to anticipate a cure.

Consider, sir, how worthless and how slight,
How destitute of counsel as of power,
Are they whom thou deliveredst from what foes,
How manifold and mighty ! These are fled
But for a moment, a brief interval,
Which should be spent in arming Syracuse
Against their fierce renewals : 'tis a time
For stern compulsion, not for compliments,
For martial training and the soldiers' law,
For him, whose sword hath rescued, to bear rule,
Not bandy with the shifting populace.
By perilous degrees this height was clomb,
To be abandoned now ! Sir, bear with me,
I know not by what argument thou seek'st
To undo all thy labour : dost thou say
This city's weak, beset by enemies,
Therefore I raze her bastion of defence ?
Her people helpless as a gasping shoal
Caught in some wave-scooped hollow, therefore I,
On whose flood only they can ride to sea,
Do ebb and leave them ? Were 't not that cold fear
Mates with Timoleon as hoar-frost with fire
By heaven I'ld think that he, whom warrior's bulk
Could ne'er make tremble, was o'ercome at last,
Out-daunted by the shadow of a shame.

TIMOLEON.

Thy counsel lacks not weight, but in the main
'Tis shot beside the mark : thou dost confound
With lawful aid usurped authority :
Not seizing this must I withhold the other ?
Who thrusts me from mine office ?   I am still
Defender of this people ; more than that,
Though Corinth's self command, I cannot be.
Thou say'st their foes are imminent : more need
That these find something worthier to defend
Than chains and degradation, and hereto
Of one they trust, to help them : but in truth
Who'ld speak of trust, while such a monstrous ' fie !'
Stands up to contradict him ? which being down,
Then first they'll know the rapture to be free,
And learn to do as freemen.   O they have had
Their fill of tyrants—will no more of them :
But should I force their loyalty, what gain ?
To be suspected, sure, betrayed, as like,—
For tyranny breeds traitors—and at last
To leave them where I found them, and give place
To some more vile adventurer, having made
No breach i' the cursèd circle.—But enough,
I overtask your patience : and yet stay ;—
The rest have spoken, or I know their minds;
But what saith Isias ?

ISIAS.

I crave pardon, sir ;
I am but a plain soldier, no wise skilled
(An I offend not with the phrase) to crack
Such nuts as these, nor aught indeed but skulls ;
Indifferent apt to govern or obey,
Where trumpets sound and armies are afield,
Nor loth to lead my fellows to the breach,
And having stormed to keep it : but for the broil
Of civil factions and the war of words—
Your learned wranglings who shall make the laws,
And whether one shall wrench, or all evade,—
I care not for such chamber-chivalry,
Nor shall not meddle with it : so being asked
Whether I count it wisdom, having won,
To keep the prize or yield it, this or that,
I square my answer to the soldier's rule,
That serves me for a better, ' might is right.'

TIMOLEON.

Sirs, I have heard your counsels ; naught remains,
But that I scrutinise their weight, and act
By what the scale determines.—Now to rest.

The Generals.

Good-night, my lord.

9

TIMOLEON.

Good-night.

[*Exeunt Generals*

—So Dion fell,
Seduced by such-like arguments, a man,
Who marred the perfect picture of a life
By one black smutch at ending.   More than he
None loathed the vice of greatness; yet he dreamed
Of arbitrary power, as 'twere a garb,
Which, made for base men, might take shape to fit
The limbs of noble action : so he doffed
The saving robe of honour, and did on
The poison that consumed him.

                    True it is
There have been upright rulers, loyal kings,
Princes yet patriots—but the time is o'er—
Who not by sufferance, but with heart's consent
Of all men, pioneered the pathless way
To freedom ; such as deemed 'twas pitiful
Being base-hearted to be born a king,
Much more by force to usurp it; who girt on
Their kinghood as a panoply of proof,
Sworn leaders of a service fraught with pain,
Not idly, as the badge of insolence
And all misdoing.   Yea, 'tis a noble dream—

To stablish judgment and do equity,
To raise the humble, not to override them,
Nursing the weak limbs of an infant state ;
To flash upon men's darkness like the dawn,
And so to soar above reproachful cloud,
Distorting fog of envy, and all taint
Of earthly attribute, as now at length
Arrived the empyræan of pure fame—
Ah ! what ?—to sink below the horizon's rim,
Droop nightward, and yield up the reins of day
To the chance hand and heady charioting
Of some rash Phaethon, to plunge in fire
Or wrench the fixèd pole !—

         Ho ! there, who knocks ?

      [*Enter* LYSIAS, *a soldier, bearing a letter.*

LYSIAS.

My lord, as one kept watch upon the wall
Some half-hour since, pacing it up and down,
He spied this letter dropped upon his path,
As 'twere from heaven.

       TIMOLEON (*glancing at it*).

         Or, say, cast up from hell ?

               [*He reads.*

' To great Timoleon, our deliverer,
Certain chief citizens of Syracuse

Send loyal salutation, and withal
Wait but the signal to declare themselves
Obedient vassals to his sovereign power,
Being ready to yield up, or, at a word,
Surprise and bind the movers of the mob,
To crush the dangerous and forestall sedition.'—
. . . So this craves instant action.—Lysias !

LYSIAS.

My lord !

TIMOLEON.

Take thou this proclamation ;
See it be cried at dawn through Syracuse,
And bid our captain of the watch come hither :
This to the late commander of the fort—
All useful arms and properties of war
To be transported hence three hours ere noon.
Yet tarry—of what temper is the night?

LYSIAS.

The night was passionate and scowling-dark,
But it is past, my lord.

. TIMOLEON.

In truth so soon?
How day forgets us in these gloomy walls!
Yon window should look east : uncurtain it ;

I·tell thee 'tis no stale or common sight—
The birth-dawn of a people.

Lysias.

Behold! my lord,
As 'twere a ship on fire far out to sea.

Timoleon.

Behold! indeed. Ay, Lysias, thou wert right;
Put out my glimmering lamp: the sun is risen!

ACT III.

SCENE III.—*The Market-place of Syracuse.*

Several months have elapsed since the events of the last scene.

1st Citizen.

'Tis twelve hours since these runagates arrived
With their ill news, and no fresh tidings yet.

2nd Citizen.

Silence proves nothing; but I fear the worst.

3rd Citizen.

And I, till worst be proved, will hope for best.
What! after all these months of prosperous toil
Since Hiketas was ousted—all things changed,
Old ills abolished, and old laws revived,
Exiles returned, and thousands come from far
To colonise and traffic, thrive and till,
When, for the poor foul trampled worm that was,
Stands up transformed, the queen of commonwealths,
This fair and virgin city—then, what then
Bid me believe these half-fed hireling knaves!

These sweepings of the shambles! who rush in,
Their swords unbloodied, and with fear-forged tales,
' Timoleon conquered, Carthage at the gates ! '—
The gods in heaven had laughed for scorn to hear.

1st *Citizen.*

Why, bravely said ; thou putt'st new heart in me :
I could believe these rascals mutinied,
And ran before the battle.

2nd *Citizen.*

Just as like :
So had their looks spoke truer than their tongues.

3rd *Citizen.*

The clamouring for arrears too jumps with that.

2nd *Citizen.*

I'll not despair till sundown : afterward—

A *Thurian Merchant.*

Would God we had ne'er set sail from Italy !
The harrying of those cursed Lucanians
Were as a happy windfall weighed with this.
Where was the conflict rumoured ?

1st *Citizen.*

Some few miles
Westward of Agrigentum, if 'tis true,

The billowy hosts of Carthage like a flood
Foamed round and overwhelmed them : these escaped
As broken spars or driftwood.

2nd Citizen.

                    While you speak,
Here are more remnants of the wreck washed in.
What news, good fellows ?

                    [*Enter Mercenaries.*

1st Mercenary.

                    No news, till we be paid :
We list not such good fellowship, nor fight
For smooth-coined phrases, but the current gold.
What ! we have served ye long enough for naught,
Poured out our sweat for your fine promises,
Who still have kept us fasting.   By the gods !
We'll have our rightful wages, and till then
Ye may go starve for tidings.

The other Mercenaries.
                    Fairly spoke.

3rd Citizen.
Hark hither, friend : if ye must sell the news
Your lives should pay for bearing, and we must buy
The knowledge of our losses, take this gold
As earnest of the gage I offer here
That ye shall have your asking.

1st Mercenary.

'Tis a bite
To stop the mouth of one man, but eked out
Among us all—no, no, we claim our own.

3rd Citizen.

To-morrow, sirs, shall ye be satisfied.

1st Mercenary.

Why then to-morrow shall ye learn the worst.

1st Citizen.

Friends, be not obdurate : but yestermorn
To 'quit your claim a levy was decreed ;
And by to-night 'twill be contributed.
Ye shall be paid to-morrow.

1st Mercenary.

Do ye swear it ?

1st Citizen.

Though every statue from his pedestal
Be plucked, and sold for the mere marble's worth.
Now what thing know ye of Timoleon ?

1st Mercenary.

The last, I trow, that ever shall be known.

1st Citizen.

How ! is he dead ?

1st Mercenary.

Ye may not doubt of it.

3rd Citizen.

Marked any that he fell ?

1st Mercenary.

No need of that,
Where one man meets a thousand.

2nd Citizen.

O brave heart !

How sped the rest ?

1st Mercenary.

We tarried not to see.

3rd Citizen.

Why fared ye then so long upon your road,
That a whole day ye lag behind the van ?

1st Mercenary.

Caught in the meshes of the mountain-ways,
When midnight was one blot, we lost the track.

ORTHAGORAS.

Wot ye of one who marched afield with ye,
A brave Corinthian leader, Æschylus ?

1st Mercenary.

Hope not for his or any man's return.

ORTHAGORAS.

Return he would not, save with victory.

1st *Mercenary.*

Plague on this droughty talking !   Come, my mates,
Here's pelf enough to make a merry night,
And many's the goodly cask, ere morning come,
Shall leak itself the lighter.   [*Exeunt.*

1st *Citizen.*

I pray heaven
Your sour lips turn the sweet wine vinegar,
To rot ye and corrode those coward bones.

3rd *Citizen.*

Had we but fifty hoplites left behind,
There's baser vintage should have flowed to-night.

2nd *Citizen.*

Alack ! these heavy tidings ! trust ye them ?

Chorus.

From far, from across the sea,
From the land of my sojourning,
I flew with a swallow's speed
On the winds of spring;
Weary of waiting as she,
When gales impede,
Beating up in the teeth of the storm on wounded wing.

Corinthian Women.

Ah, friends! though gentle seemed the breath of June,
Short was your summer; the north wind found ye soon.

Chorus.

O sweet was the sight of home
From the prow of the plunging ship!
The beat of our hearts made rhyme
      With the oar-blades' dip:
Scaling the pendulous foam,
      Or poised sublime,
Yet we shuddered no more at the curl of ocean's lip.

Corinthian Women.

O me, my heart! and better had it been
To have sunk under and be no more seen!

Chorus.

Forgot was the house of shame,
With the tale of the tears we shed,
Forgotten the long sad flight,
      . And the foreign bed:
Nothing of misery came
      To mar delight,
And the rapture hereof was alone rememberèd.

Corinthian Women.

But now thine outstretched arms appeal the skies,
And tears are gathering in those altered eyes.

Chorus.

I said, ' Lo ! the hour is come,
We have sighed for and sorrowed long : '
I filled the triumphant street
　　With a sound of song :
High rose the jubilant hum,
　　Where youthful feet
Wove a welcome of youth to that old and exiled throng.

Corinthian Women.

The mirth is hushed, the voice of pleasure mute ;
I hear a dolorous strain, without the lute.

Chorus.

As one that hath late put by
The reproach of a barren bed,
Who travailing brought forth fate,
　　And a babe born dead,
Even so bitterly I
　　With hope waxed great
Weep the loss of my longing, and am not comforted.

Corinthian · Women.

She cries on comfort, but 'tis hard to teach,
Though one gat wisdom and the gift of speech.

ORTHAGORAS.

O ye faint-hearted and wantons of your woe !
Why set ye forward to espouse Despair,
Who hath not plighted troth with ye, nor sent
To bear you to his bridal : get ye in,
Prevent not his approaching, lest ye hear
Most shameless among women.

Chorus.

                    Man, thou liest :
To that grim bridegroom I am bound this day,
And no man shall divorce us.

Corinthian Women.

                    'Tis the sign
Of a sick cause that totters to its end,
When wrath arises betwixt friend and friend.

ORTHAGORAS.

Put ye no trust in the diviner's dream ?

Chorus.

Dreams may dissemble, but the event is sure.

ORTHAGORAS.

No knot so firm but time untangles it.

Chorus.

But swifter ply the shears of Destiny.

ORTHAGORAS.

Think ye to teach, who lack the skill to learn?

Chorus.

Thy wit was clear, but God hath darkened it.

ORTHAGORAS.

There is, that shall approve thy wisdom vain.

Chorus.

Why, call aloud then! let him hear and help.

ORTHAGORAS.

It shall repent thee when thine eyes behold.

Chorus.

This were a marvel, if slain men should live.

ORTHAGORAS.

More marvellous, I wot, that God should lie.

Chorus.

I know no counsel but to wait the end.

ORTHAGORAS.

Mine eyes are full of seeing! mine ears of sound!

Chorus.

His fate were happiest being blind and deaf.

ORTHAGORAS.

The soughing of wind i' the pines!

Chorus.

Alack ! fond heart,

Here is no forest, and the streets are still.

ORTHAGORAS.

They bow themselves ! they are broke ! the storm ! the
storm !

Chorus.

Some whirlwind of distress hath caught his soul.

ORTHAGORAS.

The roof of heaven is rent with jags of fire !

Chorus.

Ye hear him how he raves and heeds us not.

ORTHAGORAS.

And from the green earth steams a sanguine sweat !

Chorus.

I tremble ; 'tis the likeness of my dream !

ORTHAGORAS.

Their wheels stick fast ; the war-steeds plunge in vain !

Chorus.

Oh, for a man's strength ! with male hands to fight !

ORTHAGORAS.

On foot they fly, their shields behind them flung !

Chorus.

The white-orbed shields ! the splendour of the spoil !

ORTHAGORAS.

But the rude spear-point pricks them shamefully.

Chorus.

My heart mistrusts him, yet the tale is sweet.

ORTHAGORAS.

The dead lie heaped ; but who shall bury them ?

Chorus.

Remains there none to deck the funeral-pyre ?

ORTHAGORAS.

Dark forms I see like phantoms come and go,
No pious hands that pay the dues of woe.

Chorus.

What seeking else ? or who the seekers ? say :
Do men ply traffic with cold breathless clay ?

ORTHAGORAS.

For trophied arms they quest and captive gold :—
Pale grows the vision— lo ! my tale is told !

Corinthian Women.

Thine art prevails not with her sore distress :
Behold her still cast down and comfortless.

Chorus.

That comfortable word, which lacks belief,
But fans to headier height the fires of grief.

Corinthian Women.

Lift up thine eyes !

Chorus.

On what new woes to look ?

Corinthian Women.

Of joy I spake.

Chorus.

All joys have I forsook.

Corinthian Women.

Oh, lift thine eyes !

Chorus.

Behold ! they are earth's to keep.

Corinthian Women.

Yet lift them.

Chorus.

Nay, they have no more tears to weep.

Corinthian Women.

Weep thou thy fill ; for joy shall find thee tears.

Chorus.

Dost thou too mock ?

Corinthian Women.

I mock but idle fears.

3rd Citizen.

Oh, lady, look ! where one comes footing fast !

Chorus.

Worst néws weighs heaviest ; therefore lags he last.

3rd Citizen.

His brows are bound with wreaths of victory !

Corinthian Women.

They shout, they sob, they clasp their hands on high.

[*Enter a Herald.*

Chorus.

Life is too solemn for such shows as this.
Three tragic pieces I protagonist
In mine own person, without mask, have played,
Sad flight, sad exile, and most sad return :
Now when for laughter at the close they call,
I have no heart to end with jollity.
Sirrah ! doth wine or madness make thee bold
To flaunt thy follies in the eye of grief ?

Herald.

Wet cheeks ! rent raiment ! and disordered hair !
Strange greeting for so glad a messenger !
If good news set thee weeping, I am gone ;
And God send one shall help thee to thy wits.

10 *

3rd Citizen.

Stay, friend: ill tidings have out-travelled thine,
And such foul breath of evils falsely blown
As with their sorrow she is half-distraught.
Speak comfort, if thou canst : thou knowest her need.

Herald.

Timoleon lives, and rides in triumph nigh.

Chorus.

O wise physician ! all my hurt is healed,
And with no mightier medicine than a word.

Herald.

He hath cut the flower of Carthage to the root.

Chorus.

O heart ! in grief thou wert all too garrulous :
Be hushed awhile, and hearken to thy joy.

3rd Citizen.

When, where, and how was this great marvel wrought ?
If strength suffice thee to tell out the tale.

Herald.

'Tis nine days since upon a misty dawn
We trod the silent summits of the height
That over-frowns Krimesus : a thick cloud
Clung to the valley-side, but from beneath
No doubtful din ascended—a dull roar
Monotonous, as of moving multitudes,

And frequent clamour, and the clash of arms,
And war-steeds fiercely neighing.   Long time we lay
Aware yet unbeholding, till at length
The vapour-veil up-torn showed brokenly
Armed spaces quick with tongues of angry light,
And a wide region populous with war.
O then the life of our great enterprise
Stood on the peril of a razor's edge ;
For Thrasius and his thousand mercenaries
Even by the fear of that appalling front,
Without a stroke, confounded, hied them home ;
Whom doubtless more were following, had not he,
Timoleon, with a shout so loud, it seemed
As if a god spake in him, seized his spear
And charged impetuous, as the mighty mass,
Surprised amidst their crossing, stood half this
Half that side of the river : fierce the shock,
At spear-length first, but after, when no thrust
Could rive those monstrous shields and plates of mail,
Foiling their fence, we pressed betwixt the files
In sword to sword encounter.   There fell down,
With huge arms cumbered, and no space to play,
The pride and flower of Carthage ; yet the weight
Of sevenfold odds rolled forward from their rear
Had haply still o'erborne us, when there pealed
A crash through heaven that split the firmament,

And from the east drove up a furious wind,
With spouting clouds and hurricanes of hail,
That scourged the foemen's faces.   Back they reeled
Blinded, and sinking in the miry slough,
Whence none arose who fell ; and checked by these
Precipitately flying, the ranks behind,
Mixed in disastrous onset friend with friend,
Broke, and were hurled into one common heap
Trampling and trampled ; while to bar their flight
The wrath-fed river reared his tawny mane
With wide jaws oped upon them : in they rushed
Pricked on by frenzy and the following spear,
Till o'er the torrent dammed and bridged with dead
We swept to spoil and slaughter.

                      Hark ! I hear
A trumpet ! 'tis the vanguard at the gates :
Who with the general, make what speed I might,
Have pressed me close at heel.   Full soon ye'll hear
From worthier lips no worser tale than mine.

Chorus.

In all thine utterance there is naught to mend,
Save that it comes too quickly to an end.

ORTHAGORAS.

Hail ! mouthpiece of a land deliverèd !
Wert thou struck dumb for ever, thou hast said.

Chorus.

O fount of sacred Hope !
That in the careful breast
Dost with sweet solace spring,
To thee I sing.
Not from the cloven crest
And haunted slope
Of old Parnassus more divinely gush
Castalia's waters, when the moonlit wave
Winds on through midnight's virgin hush
Down to the Delphian cave.
More deep thou art and inexhaustible
Than sorrow's salty well
Up-bubbling ever at thy side
Brackish and hot,
Whose source like hers is not
From tortured solitudes supplied
Rent by volcanic fires
Through bitter ashes of burnt-out desires,
But from fair fertile regions brought
Of vital impulse and heroic thought.
O thou sweet saving gift !
To every child of death
An inborn dower,
Whose taste is immortality,
Yet native as his breath !

Unloosed by thee
The fatal firm-set barriers fade and shift
Before his closing eyes ;
Yet none the less
Into the heavy air of rank excess
Thou canst not rise,
Nor send thy healing shower ;
There are who foul thee at the fountain-head
With poison-weeds of sloth ;
And rootless pride and envy's rotten growth
Choke up thy bed :—
Let this at last be said,
Where truth and constant courage bend
Their yoked necks to the steep of fate,
Thou dost the failing limbs invigorate,
And guid'st brave effort to a glorious end.

ORTHAGORAS.

Peace ! ye : the glad procession draws anigh,
And lo ! the Archons come to welcome him.

[*Enter* TIMOLEON, ÆSCHYLUS, *and other officers,
with soldiers bearing trophies of victory.*

TIMOLEON.

Men of this city, ye behold us here
Returned with triumph and fulfilled of spoil,
The kind gods favouring, and our task achieved.

Therefore to Fortune first a shrine I vow,
On whose high wall these trophies shall be hung,
And round about them be the record writ
With what great wonders she amazed and quelled
The vaunting host that dreamed our overthrow.
For never yet were myriads like to them
By mortal thousands vanquished ; but the earth
Brake up beneath them, and heaven was bowed above—
Rain, fire, and wind, and darkness ! and we heard
The sound of unseen armies, and behold !
A light of swords in the air which no man drew,
That leapt, and swept, and smote them that they fell !
And some were trampled where no war-hooves trod,
Like grass bent back beneath the blustering south !
  Wherefore be glad and give ye praise to heaven,
Seeing that for these things may no man be praised ;
For God was wroth and slew them.   But henceforth
Be shamed who fear for Syracuse : we bring
The helms and bucklers of ten thousand slain—
Phœnician marvels delicately done,
Wrought in with gold and silver ; for there lay
Their mightiest and most honourable, nor shall
The viler remnant haste them to return,
Who fled from that day's fighting.
                              Lo ! ye now,
The righteous consummation and full end

Of that which heaven appointed ! that whereto
My days of life were lengthened, when to live
Was but a burden, that of all men born
I might be richest, who was wretchedest,
And, who was banned, a blessing : for I see
Beyond my hope my noblest hope fulfilled—
A city free that wept in servitude,
And peopled that was empty, prosperous folk
Where misery sat moping, and just laws,
And patience to abide them ; and therewith
From ruinous heaps arising I behold
Her desecrated temples, and in haunts
Of old dilapidation and decay
New homes of fair contentment.   Nay, nor here
Only, but elsewhere through this altered isle
Our help hath wrought a healing, that wherein
Of all her cities raged the tyrant-brood,
That purple plague is ended, and behold !
For brute oppression and barbaric lust
The reign of laws Hellenic !

                           Yet there lives,
That till this hour hath baffled fate and doom,
Even Hiketas, who with the invader leagued,
Untaught of old disasters, burned at length
To woo belated victory ; but him
His Leontines, made bold by Carthage crushed,

Gat heart to seize, and bound, and hither hale
To Syracuse—that man must die the death.

    Next, for the recreant pack, those fangless curs,
Swift-footed, clamorous-tongued, which yelped and fled
At scenting of the quarry, these shall whine
Henceforth in stranger-kennels, where the land
Brings forth but vermin ; for not such the breed,
Men hunt the boar with here in Sicily.

    What more remains ?   I am an old man now,
And have been lustier than ye see to-day,
Though for my years full lusty ; and I would fain
Reap, ere death come, the harvest of my hand,
And taste my life's fulfilment ; for I know,
Without vainglory or swelling thoughts of pride,
That me the gods did fashion to this end
Not all as others, but on an anvil forged,
And, fanned with sevenfold blasts of love and hate,
Tried me and tempered for a sword of proof
To work their will to youward.   I do think
I have performed their bidding, and have walked
Before you all uprightly, and that herein
Ye will acquit me, as my heart acquits,
Of wrongful dealing or injurious aim,
For private ends toward any.   If this be so,—-
Nay, friends, what need of weeping ?—then would I,
Who ne'er till now played beggar, crave of you,

Yet not in guerdon, but of your good will,
One boon at my beseeching.

ARCHON.

Sir, 'tis thine :
Ask what thou wilt ; do with us as thou wilt,
Be that thou wilt ; none here shall say thee nay.

TIMOLEON.

Do ye confirm the privilege ?

People.

All, all !

TIMOLEON.

Then thus with thanks I claim it : from this hour
I cast away the burden of command,
With all its envious honours, and here stand,
Of my free choice and with the people's will,
Plain citizen of Syracuse—How, sirs !
So soon ye grudge me of your gift ? so soon
Shrink from your plighted promise ?   Nay, 'tis best :
What need we spears at home, no broils abroad ?
Were more foes yet to cope with, well ye wot
I had not stuck to serve you ; but let be ;
My wars are waged ; and not from gathering years,
But through derivèd weakness of the blood,
My sight fast fails me, and darkness draws apace :
Shall one lack eyes and lead ye ? surely no.
But I will live my residue of days

Unfeared among my fellows ; and with me twain,
A valiant soldier and a prophet sage,
Orthagoras here and Æschylus my friends,
Without whose friendship ye had scarce been free.
And if hereafter, as might well befall
Through stress of doubt or danger, ye should need
The sober insight of deliberate age
To clear false issues, or appraise the claims
Of high-contending faction, then perchance
These eyeless footsteps some good hand will guide
To the great chamber where your burghers sit
For parley ; and I will hearken their debate ;
And in the assembly shall my voice be raised,
To cheer or chide you, as an old man may.
And so—come darkness ! I'll make shift to see
The dawn of freedom upon Sicily.

Corinthian Women.

What mean ye, sisters, thus to laugh and weep ?

1st Semichorus.

Sing out for an end of woe !
   The days of sorrow are done.

2nd Semichorus.

But the light of the sun is low ;
   And darkness covers the sun.

POEMS,

BY

JAMES RHOADES.

LONDON: MACMILLAN AND CO.

1870.

Opinions of the Press.

" The bent of Mr. Rhoades's imagination seems to lie almost entirely towards a region not much frequented by the most popular poetry of the day—the region of vague emotional susceptibility, of nameless spiritual upliftings—'Ahnungen'—which bespeak an Infinite peopled with un-realised images and unfulfilled desires. It is a region of pure aspiration, not of immediate or objective experience, though the gateways into it lie through the immediate impressions of experience ; some organic sen-sation or some object of the surrounding world raising in the mind the suggestion or revelation of that other world, by an agency which what psychology can explain? Images so revealed, and desires so suggested, float dispersedly before the mind in groups of no more than incidental association, and do not get collected and combined by the reason into definite thoughts or chains of thought ; and the resulting state of con-sciousness is that which finds in music its highest and most appropriate expression. This vague or musical mood is one, it is true, characteristic of young rather than of mature poets in general ; and, taken together with his imitativeness in the matter of poetical form, might be construed as merely indicating that Mr. Rhoades is an immature writer and no more. Yet we think his readers will feel with us that this construction would be unfair in view of the self-consciousness which in his case at-tends this mood, and of the sort of success which sometimes falls to his attempts at fetching home in articulate forms to himself and us these fugitive moments of the being."—*Pall Mall Gazette*, Sept. 20, 1870.

" There is a good deal of thought scattered through these poems. . . . . The main springs of inspiration to which they owe their birth would seem to be that feeling for external nature, as for something al-most human, and that religious sense of a something behind and above nature, which are so characteristic of much of the poetry and thought of the age."—*Scotsman*, Aug. 26, 1870.

Poems, by James Rhoades.

OPINIONS OF THE PRESS—*continued.*

" If any one will read Mr. Rhoades' poetry he will soon see that there is a great deal in it to admire—much sweetness—much grace—a good deal of fine thought finely expressed in melodious verse. . . . It is difficult to particularise any of the poems; all of them have a quiet beauty of their own. . . . The sonnets . . . . are often rich in thought and beautiful in expression. . . . Mr. Rhoades concludes his volume with a dialogue betwixt Lady Jane Grey and Feckenham, a Catholic priest. It is managed with much skill, and conducted on Lady Jane Grey's side with great force and power."—*Edinburgh Courant*, Feb. 2, 1871.

" In Mr. Rhoades' poems, however, we notice at once characteristics which remove them far away from the elegant ephemera which flutter for a few weeks in the sunshine of subscribers' patronage, and then pass away to the populous limbo of disappointed verse-makers. Mr. Rhoades has evidently lived and worked in the best atmosphere of poetical influences. . . . We quote a few stanzas from a beautiful poem on the old theme of the English daisy, which has already been glorified both by Wordsworth and Tennyson. The second stanza . . . . contains a certain ambiguity of expression, otherwise this little poem, as a whole, ... is not unworthy of either of the great masters who have already touched with reverent hand the same flower. . . . We would direct particular attention to some of the sonnets, many of which have a subtle and delicate beauty and a nearness to nature that are refreshing." —*Glasgow Herald*, July 26, 1870.

" Some of the sonnets, especially, possess great power of imagery, and an elegance of diction rarely surpassed."—*Examiner*, July 16, 1870.

" The author of these poems . . . . is generally clear, has high and noble thoughts, loves nature, takes broad views of men and things, has a fine ear for music, knowledge, culture, a rare wealth of language, and that which complements all these gifts and acquirements—poetic inspiration. Not being sensational, he will not be so popular as some poets, but he must command respect, and will, I believe, win his way to a high place among the poets."—*Hertfordshire Mercury*, July, 1870.

UNWIN BROTHERS, PRINTERS, CHILWORTH AND LONDON.

www.ingramcontent.com/pod-product-compliance
Lightning Source LLC
Chambersburg PA
CBHW021113020726
47500CB00003B/740